COP HOUSE

COP HOUSE

STORIES BY

SAM SHELSTAD

 NIGHTWOOD EDITIONS

Nightwood Editions
P.O. Box 1779, Gibsons, BC, V0N 1V0
www.nightwoodeditions.com

Cover design by Angela Yen
Text design by Mary White
Printed and bound in Canada
This book has been produced on 100% post-consumer recycled, ancient-forest-free paper, processed chlorine-free and printed with vegetable-based dyes.

Nightwood Editions acknowledges the support of the Canada Council for the Arts, which last year invested $153 million to bring the arts to Canadians throughout the country. We also gratefully acknowledge financial support from the Government of Canada and from the Province of British Columbia through the BC Arts Council and the Book Publishing Tax Credit.

Cataloguing data available from Library and Archives Canada
ISBN 978-0-88971-335-2 (paper) / ISBN 978-0-88971-127-3 (ebook)

for Katie

CONTENTS

BLIND MAN

Dear lovely young woman in the small house on Fader Drive. Or—I shouldn't lie—Juliette. I know your name is Juliette. Juliette Ireland. Such a beautiful name. Is Ireland an Irish name? I hope you do not mind my leaving this letter in your mailbox. I made sure to drop it off while you were at work so as not to frighten you. I understand that it might be startling to find a stranger like myself on your porch. Especially after what happened. It was important for me to write you, however. I have three aims with this letter: one, I would like to apologize; two, I will provide an explanation; and three, I wish to extend an invitation. I will deal with these matters in that order.

First of all, I am sorry. I know what I did was inappropriate and I regret the actions I took on Wednesday night. I do not blame you for screaming, for using the bar stool to chase me out of your house or for the bruises I gathered falling down your front steps. The last thing I wanted was to hurt you and I think we can both agree that I never did *physically* hurt you. I merely—and foolishly, I know—created a misunderstanding that may have caused you to worry. Well worry no more. I feel that after you have read my explanation you will understand where I was coming from and perhaps even sympathize with me. And if you should decline the forthcoming invitation: poof! I will disappear from your life forever though the thought of this outcome pains me to imagine. Again, I'm sorry.

With that out of the way I am sure you are dying to know why I did what I did. Before we get to Wednesday night, or even that first time I surprised you while you were smoking, I need to take you back a few weeks to the night of April 21.

Did you know that April 21 is the city of Rome's birthday? It seems to me that our story beginning on the birthday of something as great and important as Rome is a wonderful omen. Anyway, it was a Saturday night and Jim Ruthers, an old colleague of mine, was in town for a conference. Ruthers and I once roomed together at McGill so we stay in touch. See? Already the picture is coming together a little more clearly: this strange man you chased out of your house is no sociopath. He has friends, they stay in touch and he went to a reputable university. So Ruthers and I convened at my apartment for a few drinks to catch up and after a couple of hours we found that my beer supply had depleted. We both agreed that our own spirits were still well stocked, however, and so decided to walk down to a bar for further refreshments and reminiscing. I rarely enjoy alcohol but I had not seen Ruthers for a few years and the two of us felt that the old college medicine might suit the occasion. We decided on Bart's Ballroom, a youngsters' hangout I am sure you are aware of due to its proximity to your own lodgings.

Normally I would prefer a more sophisticated, quiet nightspot like the supper and jazz club on Leeman but Ruthers insisted on something nearby. It was on our walk to Bart's that Ruthers suggested we play Blind Man, a game from our McGill days.

The premise of Blind Man is simple: all participants close their eyes and see who can make it the farthest towards the agreed-upon destination without looking. Back in the day Ruthers and I, full of youthful moxie, became quite adept at Blind Man. We traversed the streets of Montreal confidently and without injury, covering great distances, our eyes completely shut. That night on our way to Bart's we were a little rusty. It was good fun, however, and we eventually made it to the bar. Ruthers and I downed a couple of pints, talked about the old times and then went our separate ways. I walked home alone and on the way some mischievous force within cajoled me into playing Blind Man solo. Perhaps it was the alcohol or maybe the excitement of rekindling my student memories but please know this: under normal circumstances I would never attempt Blind Man alone. It is too dangerous. With a companion, you have someone to assist should there be an accident and the communication that goes on between two players helps paint a better picture of the surroundings. "I'm stepping off the curb," or "There is a brick wall here," add to one's own visualization of the area being sightlessly manoeuvred through. Anyway, whatever devil took over me, I went for it. And that is how I ended up in front of your house on Fader Drive.

Initially the shock I felt upon opening my eyes and finding myself in front of your house was due to having no idea where I was. I could have sworn I was on my own street which I'll let you know is several blocks from yours. Yes, it had been years since Ruthers and I were able to move confidently through Montreal without looking and I had enjoyed more drink than I usually allow myself. But I know this town and I was moving carefully and slowly. I didn't expect to land perfectly in front of my own building but I had calculated my steps so that I would at least end up on the correct street. It took me a minute to figure out where I was and when I spotted the street sign across from your house I could not believe my eyes.

Juliette, do you believe in fate? Or to be clearer, do you believe in signs? By signs, of course, I mean what people call "the universe trying to tell one something." These operate just like ordinary messages except that when you try to identify who has sent the message it appears to have randomly sprung from the chaos of existence. For example, a man on a bridge preparing to jump to his death might spot a humorous piece of graffiti on the bridge wall as he is looking down. He might start to laugh, remember why it would be better to go on living and climb down safely. The graffiti was not put there because of him—at least he did not factor into the intentions of the graffiti artist—but it was there for him. It was a sign.

I did not think anything of the incident on the night of April 21. Whatever your initial impressions of me might have been, I am not insane. When I opened my eyes in front of your house and figured out where I was, I turned around and went home.

It was the following night, April 22, that things became interesting. At work that day I couldn't stop thinking about how I had ended up so far from home despite my certainty that I had been following the proper route. After dinner I decided to walk down to Bart's and try to Blind Man my way home again. This time I would be completely sober and particularly fastidious in choosing my steps. So I went. I was sober and I was careful and when I opened my eyes expecting to see my apartment building I saw your small house on Fader Drive. I had taken the exact path as the night before. To make an error twice is one thing but for the two errors to be identical is another. I went back to Bart's and retraced my steps to your house, eyes open this time. I tried to imagine walking to my own home as I made my way towards Fader Drive but the turns, changes in elevation and even the distance were off. It didn't make sense that I should make any of the choices I would have to make to get to your house if my intention was to walk home. I stared, confused, at the exterior of your house and that was when I began thinking of signs. I hadn't even seen you yet.

That pleasure came the following week during an encounter I am sure you remember. It was exactly one week after my initial visit to your house. I was sitting at home pondering over the mystery of Fader Drive when I decided to give it another go. I walked down to Bart's Ballroom, closed my eyes and attempted to walk back home. This time I visualized two routes on the map in my mind: the route to my home and the route to yours. Whenever I made a new decision I would calculate whether it would take me towards my apartment or towards your street and chose in favour of the former. I was about to open my eyes, certain I was approaching my building, when I heard your shout. Startled, I parted my lids and saw you back away from me. You were on your porch smoking a cigarette and I was walking across the lawn towards you. You yelled, "Hey!" and I ran.

Now I can only imagine what the scene must have looked like from your perspective. You on your porch, enjoying a nice smoke when a stranger begins walking directly towards you with his eyes closed. Then you, understandably, cry out and the man, somewhat less understandably, bolts like a frightened cat. I can only hope, Juliette, that you are also able to see it from my perspective. The shock of your initial shout, the realization I was not crossing the lawn in front of my building and the suddenness of being confronted by you came all at once. It was like waking from a pleasant dream to an earthquake shaking the room. It was overwhelming and I ran on instinct. If I had had the appropriate time to process everything, of course I would have explained myself there and then. Life just isn't always as accommodating as we'd like it to be. So that was that. Now onto Wednesday night.

In the interest of full disclosure and so that any further misunderstanding might be avoided, I will admit to you that I did a little research during the interim of our initial meeting and our rather unfortunate reunion on Wednesday. While to you I was simply—and still may be—a lunatic, to me your home meant something special. It, or whatever might lie inside, was a sign. Some external force had put me there three times despite my own efforts to avoid your street entirely. So when I tell you that I went back on a couple of nights to watch your house with binoculars from across the street or that I peered through your windows and rifled through your garbage cans please note my good intentions. Even when I followed you on my bicycle to your place of work and to what I assume was your mother's house, I was not stalking you. I was merely trying to interpret the sign I had been given. I will admit that I do find you quite attractive, Juliette. I'm sure you know that you are beautiful and if you do not, damn the backwards men of this world! But my appreciation for your visual charms is one thing and my surveillance measures are another. Which brings me to the explanation for why you found me in your bathroom on Wednesday night.

To reiterate: I am not trying to justify my actions, only explain. What I did was wrong. I never should have crossed the line and entered your home. That the side window into your living room was open, however, seemed like another sign to me. I knew you were away at work and that you live alone and so my intrusion would not cause any distress. There was a recycling bin along the side of the house to prop myself up to the window, the screen popped out easily and there was nobody around to witness the act. It seemed like fate to me.

Now you know what I was doing in your house; that much should be clear. The universe was telling me that something important—something I had to see— was inside. I walked around a bit, turned on a lamp or two and surveyed the surroundings. Nothing struck me at first aside from the fact that you seemed to be a clean tasteful woman of good habits. I enjoyed the Monet prints in the hallway. I'll have to order a couple for my own apartment.

After a few minutes of innocent browsing I was hit with a sudden need to use your bathroom. Again, I'm no sociopath and the situation was causing me some stress. Breaking into strangers' homes is not something I usually do and my bowels tend to act up when I'm nervous. I realize that a bathroom is a personal space and I never would have used your facilities if was not an emergency. This is where you found me.

So we have reached the final hurdle of my explanation. Everything up to this point should make sense now except for the state you found me in when you came home early from work. You must now understand what I was doing in your home in the first place but not why you should have found me shirtless and crying on your bathroom floor, clutching your bottle of hand cream. I would have been baffled too.

One thing I've been thinking about, over and over, since the night in question is whether it was fate that brought you home from work so early. I knew from the previous week that you normally finish your shifts at the restaurant around ten or eleven. Why on this particular night would you come home shortly after eight? I'm sure there was a good reason. Maybe you were not feeling well or it was a slow night. But maybe there was also a *reason*. Maybe you were supposed to catch me.

I'm not sure what you thought I was doing and I can only imagine what leaps your mind might have made given the scene presented but here is what happened: After relieving myself I was washing up in your sink when I noticed my shirt was on inside out. This mistake has happened to you before I'm sure. While caught up in the mystery and excitement of your home and what might be waiting for me inside I left my apartment in a rush and did not notice my error. So, I took my shirt off in your bathroom with the intention of putting it back on the correct way. Before I could do so, however, I was struck by my own image in the mirror. I'm not sure exactly what it was but it felt right. There are few occasions where I find myself bare-chested outside of my own apartment and when I saw myself standing exposed in your bathroom I thought, *This is home*. Please don't take this for more than what it is. It was just a passing thought. Something felt good about looking at myself in your mirror as if I lived there with you.

Anyway, I was looking into your mirror when I noticed a patch of dry skin on my left shoulder. Nothing to be alarmed by, just something I hadn't noticed. I had switched to a cheaper laundry detergent a few weeks prior which was probably the cause. I found the hand cream above your sink thinking it wouldn't be a big deal to borrow a squirt for my shoulder. And then the scent hit my nose. It was my mother.

She was crushed by a train when I was six and I can't remember much about her—just random images and feelings. But when the smell of your hand cream wafted before me I could see her. A perfect image of my mother presented itself to me: she was wearing a green dress, sitting beside my bed, reading me a story. I could even hear her voice which I had never been able to remember before. I sat down on the floor and cried. It was a very powerful moment and through my sobs I guess I failed to hear you come in the house.

The rest of the story you already know. You came into the bathroom, probably to investigate the strange noises you heard through the door, and found the man who had approached you, blindly, the week before. You screamed and ran into the kitchen. I followed you. I was hoping to explain myself then and there but you chased me out with the bar stool. I'm sure I would have reacted the same way were we to switch places. In the commotion, I fell down your front steps but managed to pull myself up and run off. I was not aware of this at the time but in case you didn't notice I accidentally took your hand cream with me. Perhaps, subconsciously, I wanted to bring my mother home with me. And you have my shirt.

This brings us to the final matter: the invitation. You now know my side of the story and I can only hope you will trust my disclosure has been complete and honest. It may seem to you, as it did to me at first, that the sign I was given has been delivered in full. That perhaps the entire reason I was meant to find your home was to discover the cream and, in effect, a piece of my late mother. Something, call it intuition, tells me that our story is not over however. The cream is important and I will always cherish the fact that I was able to find it in your bathroom. But something about you and your house on Fader Drive still resonates with me. Maybe it was what I saw in the mirror—that feeling of being home. Don't worry, I won't break in again. I have realized my error and would never want to cause you further distress.

What I propose, instead, is that we meet. I am sure you know Wendell Park by the brewery. Meet me there on Monday afternoon at two o'clock. By the fountain. You can't miss it. I know you have the day off but hopefully you are not visiting your mother. Bring my shirt, I will bring your cream and we can talk. If you allow me I would love to keep the cream but of course it is yours and I will return it if that's what you'd prefer. If you choose to show up with a team of muscular men or even the police, I am helpless to stop you. The ball is in your court. I only hope that through reading this you have come to understand me and why I want to meet. The universe is trying to tell me something and you, Juliette, are a key part of it. I am putting my faith in you and the idea that this world contains meaning.

COP HOUSE

1

I was cutting spider shapes out of a sheet of black vinyl when John Seabreeze called me up. I remember feeling so safe when he moved in next door. After Mom died, I was having these panic attacks and then John moved in and I felt safe because he's a security guard. He works over at Pearson Airport. I was relieved because his whole career is protecting people, but then he started calling me at night and saying crazy things.

He didn't even say hello this time. When the phone rang, I put down my scissors, picked up the cordless and there was John cutting to the chase.

"I want you to come over, Ruthie," he said.

"I can't do that now."

"I want you to come over. We can play body games, Ruthie. Please. Non-sexual, I promise." He was always talking about body games, which he described as a fully clothed, free-form touching and explorative play experience. He said it was good for the heart.

"No, John. I've got the Halloween contest to work on. It's coming up."

"You'll come over. I can see you, by the way."

He hung up.

He couldn't see me, because I was in bed with the curtains shut. But that's what he did: he'd call me up, ask me to play body games and then he'd tell me that he was watching me. The funny thing is that when I passed him on the street he acted normal. Or quiet. He'd just mind his business, no mention of the calls. He had a brown moustache that looked exactly like his eyebrows—a third eyebrow above his lip.

And I believed him when he said the games would be non-sexual, good exercise and that even celebrities play them to unwind after the Oscars. But obviously it would be weird if I went over there. I really did have the contest to work on. When he called, I was lying in bed and cutting spiders out of a sheet of black vinyl for the spider cannon.

Every year my street has a Halloween decoration contest; whoever has the best-looking house wins a bucket of candy from Costco—but really it's more about the prestige. Last year I didn't win and the year before that I didn't win. The year before that, my mom was still alive and she won, and she won every other year since the contest began too. I live in her house. I grew up here. I moved away and then Mom died and now I live here in Etobicoke again.

This year I'm building a spider cannon and I have all these special tricks planned because I've got to win. I have this vision of my house decorated and it looks okay, but then I pull a switch or something and then it's suddenly amazing. I'm not sure how to do it yet. Maybe there will be orange ribbons hanging from the eavestrough, but when I pull the end of a ribbon all these yarn cobwebs fall down. I don't know. And then I can shoot off the cannon. At first I thought I'd make the spiders out of paper so they'd float around a little before they hit the ground, but then I decided on vinyl because it would be easier to gather for reloading. But I don't know. I've got two weeks—judging is on Devil's Night.

I've got to win because Mom would have wanted it that way. She always won, but now that I'm here it's Amanda P from across the street who takes home the bucket. I grew up with her. We're both strawberry blondes and we both have freckles. I look like a taller, shabbier version of Amanda P. She's so pretty. She lives in her mom's house too except her mom isn't dead— she's in a retirement home. Amanda P is married and has been to Florida several times; she really went for it and carved out a nice life for herself. She doesn't have to work because her husband has a good job at the plastics plant. I hear him yelling all the time, but that's just blowing off steam from all the plastic he has to deal with. She's got it pretty good. She can stay home all day and work on her decorations; last year she had a forty-piece orchestra of carved pumpkins playing cardboard instruments. I'm full-time at Town Drugs, so I have to work that much harder when I'm off. I'm only sleeping four hours a night until the contest is over. But it'll be worth it when I take home the prize for Mom.

You can only do so much in a day, though, so I finished cutting out a big papa spider and turned off the light. Tomorrow after work I will start thinking about the roof goblins/UFO mobile/"Coffin Express" train, etc. and how I might conceal these contraptions under a veil of mediocrity until judging.

2

The next morning, I passed John Seabreeze on the way to the bus stop. He was standing on his lawn staring up into a tree.

"Morning," I said. "What's up there—a cat?"

"Nothing," he said. He walked back inside his house.

At work, Mr. Greismeyer was hungover and in a foul mood. He's my boss. He had taken the cardigans, food containers, paystubs and *American Idol* umbrella from my locker and dumped it all in the break-room garbage bin. Said if I wanted a messy locker, he'd show me messy. Said to have some self-respect. Said I needed to at least respect Town Drugs. I'm not sure how he knew my locker combination but you don't want to mess with Mr. Greismeyer when he's hungover. One morning, I overcharged someone for a toothbrush and he made me wear a sign around my neck that said, PROBATIONARY EMPLOYEE: WATCH CLOSELY. It's hard to criticize someone like Mr. Greismeyer though. He has his own store and knows all this stuff about business. There was a lot you could learn from a guy like that. Plus, I really believe that everyone is ultimately good, my boss included. Sometimes you have to dig a little to find the good, but it's in there.

I put everything back in my locker neatly and went to set up my till. Norma, the other cashier, was already in place.

"Morning," I said.

"Fuck off, Ruth."

Norma didn't like me but she didn't like anybody else either. She hated her co-workers and she hated the customers. She regularly told Mr. Greismeyer to fuck off too, but she was his niece and he let it slide.

It was a long day. The morning was slow and dragged on and then Norma didn't come back from her lunch break. I had some big afternoon lineups but I kept it moving as well as I could. Then Jan, the other cashier, didn't show up for her shift and I had to stay until close. I left the store at eight-thirty and Mr. Greismeyer was parked out front. He had the windows down and the radio blaring techno. He saw me coming out.

"Hey, Ruth!"

"Hi sir."

I walked up to his car and looked in. There was an empty bottle of wine on the passenger seat and a half-full one between his legs. I could smell wine breath and farts.

"Baby, come join me. Let's put this morning behind us. You know who this is?"

"Sir?"

"This music, you know who it is?"

"No sir."

"I made it. On my computer at home. Pretty good, right? I call it Mr. G's Sound Explosion but that's tentative. Come on in, have a drink." Mr. Greismeyer slapped the horn and opened the passenger door for me.

"Sorry sir," I said. "It's been a twelve-hour day. Jan never showed up, you know. And I've got a Halloween contest to work on. I'll see you tomorrow."

"Suit yourself. But I want you in early, got it?"

"What, why?"

"Don't like it? Then come have a drink with me."

I left. When I got home around nine I found the word GAYBIES spray-painted on my garage door, whatever that meant. And someone had dug up my petunias and stuffed them in the mailbox. There are a lot of teenagers in my neighbourhood—my backyard shares a fence with the high school football field. But this new attack was no biggie because I could cover the graffiti with Halloween decorations and the petunias were going to die soon anyway. I went inside, made an egg bagel and pulled out my crafting pail. There was work to do.

3

I had trouble sleeping that night despite exhaustion. I turned in around one after constructing two Coffin Express train cars out of cardboard boxes and drawing up plans for a mummy conductor but I couldn't settle down. First of all, John Seabreeze kept calling. I unplugged the phone at one point and then I heard a scratching at my front door. I looked out my bedroom window and saw a big shadow run into John's house. Also, I couldn't stop thinking about those teenagers or whoever spray-painted my garage. Why would they do that? What is GAYBIES?

One of the great challenges of the Halloween contest is the constant vandalism on my street. Last year I made a life-sized zombie out of papier mâché and one of my mother's old pantsuits, and someone ripped the head off and took a shit inside of it. But these kids won't touch Amanda P's yard because they're all scared as hell of her husband who looks like a Neanderthal. Wish I had that kind of security. I mean, there's John Seabreeze next door but he's so skinny. Even with three eyebrows, or three moustaches, even with his pressed uniform and aviator shades it's not enough to command the respect of these hooligans. Although maybe it isn't fair to call them hooligans. It's a teenager's nature to rebel. These kids have it rough what with puberty and bullying and exams. They may act out but there's a puffy layer of goodness beneath. You can be sure of that.

So while I was lying in the dark not sleeping—pretty much waiting for my seven o'clock alarm to go off—I thought of the cop house. When I was eight my dad started hitting Mom so Mom and I moved from our quiet street in Etobicoke to a sketchy neighbourhood in the city. I didn't like that there were people everywhere and I didn't like the way they looked. They were always shouting at night—I could hear it from my bedroom—and I was scared all the time. Then one day my mom pointed out this house at the end of our street. She said it was a cop house and that I needn't be afraid because the police were right there and if anything went wrong they would help us out. Mom was telling me that a police officer lived in the house but at the time I thought she meant all the police officers lived there. I pictured them eating meals at a big long table and watching television together. I could see these cops lined up in the upstairs hallway, towels around their waists and holding bars of soap and hair gel, waiting for the shower. And it worked: I stopped being scared. I loved living near the cop house.

Later I found out it was just Officer Kearn in there—who I think lost his badge for Tasering his wife—and we eventually moved back to the suburbs but the idea of the cop house stuck with me. Whenever I feel unsafe I just imagine all these police officers living together in a little house and I calm right down.

So that's what I did. I thought about the cop house, relaxed a little and eventually I fell asleep. I may have even dreamt about the cop house but maybe I was just thinking about it and I'm confusing the thinking with the dreaming.

4

I had a busy afternoon at the drugstore and Mr. Greismeyer was hungover again. He kept knocking over my candy bar display and calling me a dipshit but Jan showed up for her shift and I got to go home at four-thirty.

I began work on the mummy conductor. I wrapped toilet paper around a big teddy bear, made him a conductor's hat out of felt and then started on the light display for the roof. I wanted it to say BOO in white lights, but then I'd turn on a different set of orange lights and the letters would become the eyes of these elaborate jack-o'-lanterns with speech bubbles coming from their mouths that said BOO in smaller letters. And then I'd turn on another set of red lights and the little letters from the speech bubbles would be smaller jack-o'-lantern eyes and so on but I only had enough lights and nails for one BOO. I was untangling the lights in my bed when I smelled smoke.

I looked out the window, saw the smoke coming from my front yard and ran downstairs and onto the porch. It was the Coffin Express. Through the flames I saw a pair of bicycles peel around the corner at the end of the street and disappear. I ran over to the side of the garage, turned on the faucet and doused the fire with Mom's hose. Last stop for the Coffin Express! I almost said this little joke out loud to lighten the mood but John Seabreeze was staring at me from his window and I went back inside.

I returned to untangling the lights for the roof because you can't let little setbacks get in your way. Gotta keep moving. But then I started feeling angry and I broke one of the little plastic light casings in my fist. I decided to make an egg bagel.

I ate in front of the TV and at first I was excited because Martha Stewart was on. She's just so good.

But it turned out to be a commercial and then it went back to the news which I can't watch. Too depressing. Especially world news which is always conflict and crying mothers and animals covered in black goop— but local news can give me anxiety too. I changed it to the weather channel and ate my egg bagel in peace.

After eating, I returned to the lights and started having doubts. Like, why bother untangling these lights? Why bother entering the contest at all? Would my life improve dramatically if I won the bucket? No it would not. I would still work at the drugstore and live amongst teenage arsonists and be lonely all the time. My pillow would still smell like tears every morning, if tears left a smell.

But you can't think like that. That kind of thinking gets you nowhere so I untangled the lights and got out the ladder. I spent two hours up on the roof arranging the lights and I had to put a flashlight in my mouth because it was dark but I did it. The lights spelled out BOO and it looked amazing. Even without the secret jack-o'-lantern eyes and everything. Because once you give up on something like a little contest then you start questioning everything else in your life. Why bother going to work today? Why bother putting on antiper-spirant? Why get out of bed at all? And that's pathetic. We need these contests—things to really strive for—to keep us going and so I resolved to win the Costco bucket no matter what. Let the teenagers set fire to my actual house. I'll use it to my advantage and make my theme Partially Burned-Down Home with Ghost Firemen.

"Look out, Amanda P.," I said in the direction of Amanda P's house. "Your old pal Ruth is on the warpath."

5

The next day I had so much positive energy I didn't mind that someone threw up on the floor by the Gatorade and I had to clean it. It didn't even bother me that Mr. Greismeyer ate the sandwich I brought and then made me spend my lunch break vacuuming his car. I almost lost it when I saw a kid bike by the window wearing my felt conductor's hat but I reminded myself that it didn't matter. That it was just a hat and that he was just a kid. He might grow up to be a famous doctor and help cure diseases. Deep down he was probably a little angel and there was no need for me to get upset so I didn't. I was focused on the contest; I had so many ideas.

For one, I decided to rebuild the Coffin Express because it would definitely impress the judges and we had lots of diaper boxes in the back of the store I could use. I also came up with this genius plan to put a kind of lever underneath the candy bowl on my porch so when trick-or-treaters reached in they'd push the bowl down on the lever and a fake arm would come out from underneath the table and touch their legs. My creativity levels were through the roof.

Jan didn't show up for her shift and I had to stay until close again. I was still beaming though. So much so that when I left the store and heard techno blaring from Mr. Greismeyer's car in the parking lot I decided to join him for a quick drink. He was always so nice in the evening. When you catch a normally grumpy person in a good mood it's important to soak them up and show them how much you appreciate their positive side. Then they'll try to be in a good mood more often. It's true.

"That's a girl, Ruthie," he said, pouring wine into a Pepsi can for me. "You know, I always thought you had it in you."

"Thanks, Mr. Greismeyer."

"Goddamn right it's time you joined me in here. In my car bar. Goddamn it's nice to sit down and have a drink like this."

"It's very nice."

We sat listening to the techno for a while which wasn't really that bad.

"You know, if I wasn't a married man," he said, peeling at the label on his wine bottle, "I'd be all over a girl like you. Goddamn right. You've got some baby fat on you, for sure. But I love it. All the right places, you know?"

"Thanks." I meant this too. Perhaps what he'd said was borderline inappropriate but he was essentially just complimenting me. There's always room in the world for compliments.

"But don't get any ideas in your head now alright? I've got a wife waiting for me at home. She's insane."

"Yes sir."

"That's right. Now get the hell out of my car before I do something that's out of line."

I left. I missed the last bus and had to walk home but I had a nice buzz and the stars were out. I mean, I only drank half a Pepsi of wine but I really felt like I was buzzing. I stopped to pet a cat that was lying in the middle of the sidewalk and it licked my hand. My hand smelled like milk. A few minutes later I found a piece of pink chalk in someone's driveway. I wrote GAYBIES on the curb and ran away. I laughed to myself. I felt so young.

And then I got home. The lights I had hung were pulled from the roof and thrown into the street. My living room window was broken too and when I went inside I found a rock with a note tied to it. The note said, BOO YERSELF BITCH.

I screamed.

6

When I was done screaming I realized the phone was ringing and answered it. John Seabreeze, of course.

"I heard you," he said.

"I'm sorry, John. I'll be quiet now."

"No, that's not..."

"It's these kids. These darn kids, these fucking kids." I was crying and talking at the same time. Maybe it was the wine. Or maybe it was the awful things that were happening but either way I was crying.

"You sound tense. If you want to come over, we could..."

"If you say anything about body games, I swear to God, John. Jesus."

"But just so you know, you'd calm right down. Worries out the window. Jennifer Aniston? That's how she got over Brad."

"Hey, did you see who did it? You were home, right? Did you see anything?"

"No."

"Nothing?"

"Sorry."

"I'll tell you something. You catch these kids for me and I'll come right over. Body games all night, whatever you want. Catch these kids and I'm in."

"Really?"

"Really."

He hung up.

I got the broom and swept up the glass from the window. I threw out the note and the rock and retrieved my BOO lights from the street. It looked like most of the lights were broken but I put them in the closet and not the garbage because maybe they'd be useful for something else. Like Medusa hair? Is she a Halloween thing?

I went to make an egg bagel but I was out of both eggs and bagels so I had the last swig of milk and went to bed. There was plenty of work to do still but my eyes kept closing. That's why you shouldn't drink alcohol during contest season: lesson learned. Stay sharp. While I was turning off the hall light I looked out the window and saw John Seabreeze standing on his porch in the dark.

7

The next morning, I woke up early and pulled out the crafting pail. For the UFO mobile, I decided to make one big spaceship that would deploy three smaller ships from its base when a switch was pressed. These three ships would each deploy three even smaller ships which would then drop little Plasticine aliens with parachutes. I'd press the switch during judging and illuminate the whole scene with a green spotlight. And a tape would be playing—some kind of eerie hum. Yes.

I was running out of supplies so I bussed it down to the dollar store. I bought yarn, twine, elastics, paper clips, construction paper, transparent paper, toilet paper, markers, watercolour paints, Plasticine, glue sticks, scotch tape, duct tape, cotton balls, pie plates, plant pots, Tupperware containers, plastic cups, felt and two Oh Henrys. I steered clear of the Halloween section—that's cheating—and dragged my bulging plastic bags to the second-hand store where I bought three flashlights, a cape and a real farmer's pitchfork. I had to call a cab to take everything home and there was an embarrassing moment when I called the driver "Mom" but thankfully she just laughed.

As I was bringing the supplies to the porch Amanda P gave me a whistle. I put everything down and went across the street. She was digging a pit.

"Hi Amanda," I said. "What are you digging there? A pit?"

"What kind of stupid question is that?"

"No, I mean is it for the contest?"

"I'm digging my way to fucking China," she said. She was in a mood, which was fine. She had a green bruise that looked like a slug crawling under her left eye. "Why don't you take the shovel for a while? I'm swamped and I know you've got the day off. My back feels like shit."

"But Amanda? I kind of have a lot to do myself. With the contest."

"Oh really? *You've* got a lot to do? For Christ's sake just help me out and be a good neighbour for once. My back, Ruth."

Before I could respond, Amanda's front door swung open and her husband came out. He glared at me.

"The damn remote control," he growled.

"I'll be right in, dear," Amanda said. "Ruth?"

"Sure, I'll take over for a little while," I said. "Go rest your back."

I helped dig for two hours and then snuck off to work on my mobile. I was sweaty and craved a nap but I kept at it. I made these amazing spaceships out of the construction paper and Tupperware containers—especially the mother ship, which had portholes with little googly eyes looking out of them—but couldn't figure out how to make them pop out of each other via a switch. I just left it all hanging out like a jellyfish and it looked beautiful. I was proud of myself. So maybe I didn't need these gimmicks; the elegance of the finished mobile transcended the elaborate presentation I originally had in mind. It was all it needed to be. I hung it on the porch.

Later I saw Amanda P filling her pit with naked baby dolls, which was maybe going too far. But then again, she's the seasoned pro. Perhaps the judges appreciate her willingness to take risks which is pretty inspiring but it was getting late and I was tired from all the shopping and crafting and pit digging. I looked at my mobile once more and went to bed.

8

My phone rang at two-thirty in the morning. I knew it was probably John Seabreeze but it might have been an emergency so I picked up. It was John Seabreeze.

"Alright, Ruth," he said. "You can come on over."

"It's two-thirty in the morning. I'm not playing body games with you in the middle of the night. You have to quit..."

"No it's not body games. Some kids came by your house a few minutes ago."

"What?"

"They were going for that thing hanging on your porch. I stopped them."

"They were? You did?"

"And two of them got away. One of them didn't."

"What happened to the kid that didn't get away?"

"Come on over, Ruthie."

I went over. I knocked on the front door but John

came around the side of his house and led me into the back. There was a light on in his tool shed.

"Is that..."

"He's in there alright. Little shit. Come look."

"I can't believe it," I said. It felt like a dream. It wasn't a nightmare really but it also wasn't one of those really good dreams where it's your birthday and the presents keep coming.

"Don't be shy. He's not going anywhere," John said.

I peered into the little window and saw the kid who had biked by the drugstore the other day. The one who wore my conductor's hat. He was sitting on the floor and crying. John banged on the side of the shed and the kid started crying even louder.

"You kidnapped him," I said. My mouth was dry and I felt heavy like I would sink into the grass. "You have to let him go."

"You said to catch him," John said. "I caught him. And besides, I gave him a choice. Told him he could sit in there until I felt he was ready to come out or I could call his parents. He made his decision. Here, try banging on the wall. He goes nuts."

"You have to let him go."

"I will, I will. But give the wall a little bang with your fist. Give it a try first."

"Let him go now, John."

"Fine. But I'm telling you..." John went to unlock the door but I stopped him.

"Wait," I said. "Wait until I'm home first."

As I was walking back to my house I heard a loud

bang followed by a kind of moaning. It might have been the kid crying but it might have been my stomach too. All I had to eat that day was two Oh Henrys. I was hungry and tired and had work in the morning so I went back to bed. The kid would be fine; John would let him go. Everything would be fine. John was actually pretty good at catching vandals when motivated. My mobile was hanging on the porch—not a scratch on it.

9

The next evening Jan didn't show up for her shift and I stayed until close. Mr. Greismeyer was parked out front when I left. He called me over.

"Ruthie, come have a drink. I've got a new track to show you. And I brought you a cup from home this time."

"I can't," I said. "Sorry sir. Another long day. It's late and I have the contest to work on." I hated to disappoint him and it was nice of him to invite me into his car again but there was so much to do. I couldn't afford to lose focus.

"Goddamnit, get in here."

"I'm sorry sir."

"Goddamnit, I brought you a cup."

I left. I caught the last bus and on the way home from my stop I was startled by a noise coming from Amanda P's yard. A raccoon was rummaging around in the baby pit. I watched it for a minute and then noticed a man hanging from the tree in her yard. There was a rope around his neck and his entrails were pouring out from his stomach. It was, of course, a dummy—the entrails were coloured socks. A strange new direction for Amanda P but it definitely showed creativity. There was a sign stuck to the dummy's chest too. I came closer, scaring off the raccoon, so I could read it. The sign said, CHILD MOLESTER.

My own decorations, for a change, had been left alone. The mobile was hanging unscathed on my porch as was the BEWARE OF GHOST banner I had stuck to the garage door to cover the graffiti. No rocks, no notes, no nothing.

I went inside and the phone was ringing.

"So," John Seabreeze said. "I think it's time for some games."

I hung up and went over. What could I do? I owed him.

He didn't look at me when he answered the door and he kept rubbing the back of his head. He was wearing a grey sweatsuit with the shirt tucked into the pants and the pants tucked into the socks.

"Take off your coat and your shoes," he said. "You can leave the rest on."

I took off my coat and shoes and he led me into the basement. There were candles lit all around the room. Blue gym mats lay across the floor.

"So how do we do this exactly?"

"I'll get us going," he said. "Lie down on your back."

I got on my back and John started dragging me around the mats by my feet. It was kind of fun actually.

Then he got down on his knees and started hugging my legs. He was squeezing them pretty hard but it didn't hurt. It wasn't so bad.

He hugged my legs for a bit then asked if there was anything I'd like to try. I said I couldn't think of anything but he kept on pressing so I said that maybe we could try kissing. I mean John looked pretty good in his sweatsuit and he was a talented security guard and I hadn't kissed anyone for a long time but he said I was missing the point. Then he turned me over on to my stomach and grabbed me around the waist. He began walking around on his knees so that my chest and face slid across the mats in front of him. Like he was cleaning the mats and I was his rag. The mats smelled like Windex.

Things went on like this for almost an hour and then I excused myself. I was so tired and I hadn't eaten all day. I thanked him for helping me out with the teenagers and he thanked me for the body games. He said I was great. I tried to kiss him good night but he closed the door and I went home.

10

That night I dreamt about the cop house except it wasn't a nice dream. I'd say it was almost a nightmare. In the dream all these policemen were dragging me around their house by my feet. They were taking turns and sometimes they would bang me into a wall. Then one of them let me fall down the stairs into the basement and they closed the door on me. It was so dark. I woke up all sweaty and it was dark in my house too.

The next morning I called in sick to work which was only a half-lie. I was just tired. I slept in and spent the day working on the contest. I felt guilty because I was supposed to be at the store but it was worth the guilt because I got so much done. I used a bicycle pump, a funnel and a piece of window screen to finish off the spider cannon which worked perfectly. I made so many cotton cobwebs and put them everywhere. More banners, more orange ribbons. A new conductor's hat for the mummy. I painted a black cat on the lower sash of my front window and two red circles on the upper sash so that when you opened the window the lower sash aligned with the upper sash and the cat suddenly had scary red eyes. I worked all day and when I went to bed my decorations were still standing. The vandals had backed off. I was safe.

Then John Seabreeze called me up in the middle of the night.

"I caught another one Ruthie."

I went over. I met him in the backyard. The light was on in his tool shed again.

"Don't be alarmed," he said, "but this one's a little older."

"How much older?"

I peered through the little window. It was Mr. Greismeyer. He had a scarf wrapped around his mouth and he was lying on the floor. He was tied to a chair, which had tipped over.

"What the hell? What…"

"He was sneaking around your house. Do you know this man?"

"That's my boss, Mr. Greismeyer."

"Shit."

We went inside and I untied the scarf.

"Goddamnit Ruth," Mr. Greismeyer said. "Is this psychopath your friend or something? Go call the police."

John Seabreeze helped him up and untied him. Mr. Greismeyer was frantic. He yelled at John and shoved him into the grass. He yelled at his lawyer who wasn't there. Then he yelled at me. I went home and called the police. I was crying on the phone but the man I spoke to was nice and two officers eventually came. They asked John all kinds of questions and made Mr. Greismeyer sit in his car until they finished because he kept interrupting. I had to answer a lot of questions too but I wasn't in any trouble. I made the officers coffee and egg bagels. I also made Mr. Greismeyer an egg bagel but he threw it on the ground.

"You know, I was coming to check on you," he said. "I knew you weren't sick, you stupid liar."

"I'm sorry sir," I said.

"Yeah well you can put that on your goddamn resume because you're sure as hell fired."

John went back inside. There was nothing the police could do since he was just trying to protect his neighbour. Mr. Greismeyer was furious. As everyone drove away I saw Amanda P looking out her window at me. I waved and she ducked out of view. The light in her window went off and I stood on my porch waiting to see if she'd come back but she didn't. I could hear the raccoon digging around in her pit.

11

While I wasn't exactly thrilled I had lost my job it couldn't have been better timing. I now had a week of distraction-free contest prep time and I took full advantage of the opportunity. When life gives you lemons, make a lemonade stand with little scarecrow children proprietors attached by string to the lemonade jug so that when someone pours a glass of lemonade the children stand up to collect payment.

I crafted like hell the whole week. I woke up early, stayed up late, and my fingers turned black from glue bits and markers. I hung white towels from the tree and attached little paper hats and glasses to them so they looked like gentleman ghosts. I found a floodlight in the basement which I used to illuminate the UFO mobile—it looked perfect. I carved pumpkins, made mini-tombstones for the garden, hung ribbons pretty much everywhere and cut skeleton silhouettes out of cardboard and painted fun glow-in-the-dark faces on them. The Coffin Express was new and improved and the lemonade stand was a perfect introductory piece at the end of the driveway. I didn't have a distinct theme like Amanda P did—her grotesque, envelope-pushing, gore décor now included heads on pikes and a lifelike lawnmower accident scene—but everything in my yard looked nice in a classic Halloween sense. I worked hard and I was proud.

The kids left me alone too. I was worried they'd come back and inflict even worse damage on my decorations now that I was ignoring John (since the incident with my boss I decided it would be best to avoid any further distractions) but the neighbourhood was quiet. In fact, when I passed teens on my way to the store they'd cross to the other side of the street. There must have been rumours going around.

Mr. Greismeyer made a few appearances. He'd park on my street at night and drink in his car. I think he wanted me to come out and sit with him but I stayed inside. I didn't want to encourage him. I had work to do.

I kept my focus on the contest but it didn't really matter in the end. When Devil's Night came, Amanda P won the bucket. She deserved it, really. She took such a huge risk with her theme. I thought the judges, who were mostly old women, would find her display too disturbing. Even I was creeped out and couldn't look at her lawn without clenching my teeth a little but it shows you how the judges based their decisions on artistic merit. Amanda was a true artist. There was so much I could learn from her. When they said her name, everyone clapped for a full minute. I joined in of course. I think I clapped the loudest. I waited in line to shake Amanda's hand and congratulate her on the big win, then went home. I was exhausted. I sat on my couch thinking I'd just rest for a minute and reflect on the day but I tipped over and fell asleep.

It was dark outside when I woke up and my stomach made noises. I went to make an egg bagel but my hands were trembling and I dropped all the eggs. The whole carton hit the kitchen floor and all the eggs broke. I grabbed a cloth and started wiping up the mess but I guess I was crying because I couldn't see too well and my hands were still trembling. I just kind of spread the eggs around and then I started yelling. I'm not sure what I was yelling exactly but it was probably something to do with Amanda P because that's who I was thinking about. It was all a blur.

Basically, I was thinking about how she had won the contest but that it wasn't fair because her display was gross while mine was family-friendly. How Amanda's yard was frightening the neighbourhood kids and my yard was only spooky in a fun way and it wasn't fair. How nothing is ever goddamn fair and people like Amanda waltzed around receiving candy for psychologically damaging little children. I kept yelling until my throat stung. My hands were covered in eggshells. It felt like I wasn't in control of my body, that it was just doing things on its own. I went into the craft cupboard and gathered up all my paint tubes and put them in a shopping bag. I checked the label of Lake Placid Blue to make sure that the brand was flammable and then I went into the kitchen and grabbed the barbeque lighter. I put on my boots and went outside.

The contest festivities were over and the street was

empty. I was in a state or possibly a trance. I walked over to Amanda P's yard and squirted paint into her baby pit. I squirted and squirted and threw the empty tubes into the pit as well. The baby dolls were covered in a rainbow topping of paint squirts. I pulled out the barbeque lighter and was about to ignite everything when I heard shouting from inside Amanda P's house. I ran home and locked the door.

The shouting had jolted me out of the trance. In my house I felt like myself again, like I was in control, which meant I also felt shame. Why would I ruin Amanda P's baby pit? She had won fair and square. Good thing I was stopped before I lit the pit up. And the most shameful thing of all was that I also felt good—like I noticed this warm feeling deep inside me over what I'd done and what I'd planned on doing. Like a part of me was proud of the paint squirts. This made me feel even more ashamed. I paced around the house, focusing on my shame and ignoring my secret pride until I tired myself out and lay down on the couch again. I fell asleep with my boots on.

12

I woke up to the sound of a man shouting in the street. I looked out the front window. It was Amanda P's husband.

"Yeah run away, you ungrateful bitch!"

He stood on their front porch with a bottle in his hand. Amanda P was running across the street to my house. When I went to unlock the front door she was already pounding on it.

I let her in and made tea for us. We sat on stools in the kitchen. She was shaking and had a fat lip.

"Are you okay?" I asked. "What happened?"

She didn't respond.

We sipped our tea and listened to the clock tick until Amanda P said she was hungry. I got the Halloween candy bowl down from the mantle and she ate a snack-sized Oh Henry.

"I'm scared," she said. She was really shaking.

I told her about the cop house; how there was this little house only a block away from our street where all the police officers lived. That they wore their uniforms while they did chores and had special blue cop pajamas with red stripes down the side. That they had barbeques and laughed and watched the weather channel together. That they had a heated pool in the backyard and did cannonballs.

"What about their wives?" Amanda P said. "Or husbands?"

"The spouses get to stay. And the children too. They all live in the house together."

"Do they have their own bedrooms?"

"No," I said. I struggled to keep my eyes open, but it was important that I hide my fatigue. I needed to be there for my friend. "They sleep in one big bedroom on the second floor. They have bunk beds. And every night, once all the cops and their families are under their blankets and the light is off, they sing a song together. A good night song."

"But what if there's a crime?"

"I'm sorry?"

"What if there's a crime at night while all the cops are asleep?"

"The crimes only happen in the day," I said. "Because the criminals need to sleep too."

"Jesus, Ruth," Amanda P said. "What the hell is wrong with you?"

But she wasn't shaking anymore. She wasn't shaking at all.

I took her up to my old bedroom, plugged in the dehumidifier and brought her a glass of milk. She went to sleep and I stood in the doorway. She looked so vulnerable lying there. The only thing protecting her from the frightening world outside Mom's house—*my* house—was me. I was in charge.

As I watched my friend sleep, the gloss on her fat lip catching the moonlight that shone through the window, I knew everything would be fine.

NEW ICE KINGDOM

Things different in New Ice Kingdom, but things also same. Things same: snow, water, ice, ice holes. Spend most of time at ice holes. Sun come during day as always, then go away at night. Things different: not as many polar bear—just me. That mean no Bud, Bud my son. Miss Bud. Not so much miss others.

Also different: not good at killing seal. Before was good at killing seal.

To kill seal, first find ice hole. Wait by ice hole, maybe for long time. When seal comes up for air, there is smell of seal's breath. When smell seal's breath in hole, reach down and kill seal by biting head. If flopping, bash with paw. When seal dead from head bite/bashing, drag to nice spot, eat. Or, if not hungry, bury in secret spot for later.

Was very good at this in Old Ice Kingdom. Ate lots of seal, gave seal bits to son, Bud. Also gave seal bits to other, less-good seal killers like Maury, who is mooch. Since come to New Ice Kingdom, not so good at killing seal. Hesitate. New Ice Kingdom has ice holes and seals, seals swim to ice holes for air; all normal. But when smell seal breath now, not quick. Hesitate. Seal go back down.

Last meal? Long time ago; sun come and go away one hundred times or more. So, hungry.

Today, maybe good day. Optimistic. Find ice hole, lay down. Wait at ice hole. No seal breath. Wait long time, then go away. Find new ice hole.

At new ice hole, lay down. Wait at ice hole. Wait very long time and when about to go away: seal breath. Hesitate. Seal go back down.

Hungry.

Later, Sun go away. While Sun going away, thank Sun for day. Even though not good day—no catch seal. But not Sun's fault. Maybe tomorrow better. Dig small pit in ice, sleep.

◆

Today, meet friend. No friends in New Ice Kingdom until now. Was at ice hole waiting for seal breath. Waited long time, then smelled seal breath. Hesitated. Seal go back down. Then heard noise. Turned around, saw fox. Thought was Bud at first—same size, colour— but not Bud. Fox.

Fox looked hungry—wanted seal bits? But no seal so walk away. Would have given fox seal bits, because fox friend, but no seal. So fox go away.

Later go to different ice hole. Lay down, wait. No seal breath. Wait long time, no seal breath. See fox in distance, waiting for seal bits, but no seal. Fox go away.

Decide to spy on Old Ice Kingdom. Have to be sneaky because of Maury. Walk long time, see Old Ice Kingdom across water. Big swim from New

Ice Kingdom to Old Ice Kingdom; water gap good boundary. Hide behind snow pile near shore, look at Old Ice Kingdom. See Bud. Bud with Maury. Bud Maury's son now? No, Bud still my son. Miss Bud. Not so much miss Maury.

Hear noise, look back—fox. Fox followed. Fox good, fox friend. Maybe fox thinking about seal bits. But not killing seal now; spying on son and Maury. Good team, me and fox. Sidekicks. Will call fox "Foxy," go on adventures, kill seal and give Foxy seal bits. Foxy and Bear.

Fall asleep on snow pile. Wake up, Bud gone. Maury gone. Foxy gone. Go back to New Ice Kingdom.

Hungry. Tired.

Sun go away. Thank Sun for day. Thank Sun for Foxy. Today good day because have new friend. Also bad day because no seal. Dig small pit in ice, sleep.

◆

Adventure for Foxy and Bear today.

After Sun comes, go to ice hole, wait. Wait long time, smell seal breath. Hesitate. Seal go back down. Hear noise, see Foxy. No seal bits, sorry. But still friends. Go to look for different ice hole, maybe better luck. Walk for long time, see thing far away. Maybe seal? Sometimes seal sit on ice, rest. This good.

Sneak up on seal behind snowdrift. Foxy following. Get close. Peer over drift at seal, ready to attack. But not seal. Not look like seal, not smell like seal. Get closer: shit. Own shit from different day. While walking away to find ice hole, see Foxy go over to shit pile. Foxy eat part of shit. Good adventure.

Then at ice hole waiting for seal breath and thinking of Bud. Miss Bud. Bud miss me? Not know.

Miss own dad. Showed how to wait by ice hole, kill seal. Remember Dad giving water rides. Would hold onto Dad's neck/back, then Dad would swim around in water between Old Ice Kingdom and New Ice Kingdom. Didn't go to New Ice Kingdom though because Dad made frowny face and pointed paw at New Ice Kingdom to say, There not good. Old Ice Kingdom good. But New Ice Kingdom not so bad. Except hungry. Not good at killing seal in New Ice Kingdom.

Want Bud back, but Bud maybe not want back. Because messed up. Did bad thing, now Bud not happy.

While thinking of Bud and own dad, smell seal breath. Hesitate. Seal go back down.

Sun go away. Thank Sun for day, thank Sun for Foxy. Dig small pit in ice, sleep.

◆

Today very desperate. Hungry. Almost did bad thing.

When sun came, went to ice hole. Foxy near, waiting for seal bits. Waited, smelled seal breath, hesitated. Seal go back down.

Hungry.

Went to secret spot, dug up secret thing. This not

good. Should not dig up secret thing. But hungry, so did. Secret thing still there, buried deep in snow. Same: bite marks on head, but good condition. Very hungry, but want to be good dad for Bud, so put back. This very hard to do, because of hungry. Put secret thing back in secret spot. Went to ice hole.

Wait at ice hole, no seal breath. Foxy watch then go away.

Sun go away. Thank Sun for day, thank Sun for Foxy, thank Sun for Dad who taught to be good and not eat secret thing. Dig small pit, sleep.

◆

Today not good day. Hungry. Do not leave pit. Should probably go to ice hole with Foxy, but tired. Sun looking down like, Why still in pit? Why not go to ice hole and try again? But still not get up.

In pit, thinking of Old Ice Kingdom. Miss Old Ice Kingdom. Miss Bud. Remember being cub, Bud's age, playing ice hole game. So much fun when cub. Would go with friend, find two ice holes near each other. Would dive into first ice hole, swim in water under ice until come out of second ice hole. Scary because what if couldn't find other ice hole. But always did because smart. Learned ice hole game from Dad. Dad was good dad. Later, taught ice hole game to Bud, so good dad as well. Except ice hole game how bad thing happened. So maybe not good dad now.

Thinking about bad thing, feel bad for Maury.

Although feel bad for self because miss Bud. At least Bud still here. Maury's son not here. Because of bad thing.

Remember was waiting by ice hole in Old Ice Kingdom. This was before, when good at killing seal. Bud nearby, playing ice hole game with Maury's son. Bud and Maury's son best friends.

Was waiting, then heard noise in ice hole. Smelled breath.

Did not hesitate.

Reached down with paw, grabbed seal, bit head.

Not seal.

First thought was Bud, very scary, but not Bud. Thank Sun. But, was Maury's son. Not good. Bud run over, see best friend with blood on head. See Dad with blood on mouth. Bud cry. This very bad. Bud run off—scared of own dad? Not chase after. When Maury find out, maybe Maury try and kill one who bites son's head. So take Maury's son in mouth, run away. Swim across to New Ice Kingdom, bury Maury's son in secret spot. Not good dad like own dad.

Sun go away. Thank Sun for day, even though whole day in pit. Hungry. Bad thoughts.

◆

Today good? Today bad? Not know.

Today good because when Sun comes, leave pit, make decision. Go over options: Since not good at killing seal in New Ice Kingdom, will die if stay in

New Ice Kingdom. Because hungry. And since killed Maury's son with head bite, will die if go to Old Ice Kingdom. Because maybe Maury want revenge. So stay in New Ice Kingdom and go to Old Ice Kingdom are same thing. Will die.

But, come up with plan: If go to Old Ice Kingdom, can bring secret thing. Dig up Maury's son from secret spot, bring to Old Ice Kingdom, then Maury and Bud see: he dying because hungry, but he not eat Maury's son. Even though hungry, even though dying. Still not eat. So he good, he accident, he sorry.

Today bad because when go to secret spot, secret thing dug up. See Foxy eating secret thing close to secret spot. Angry. Chase Foxy. Foxy fast but Foxy stop to throw up and then catch Foxy. Snap neck. Snap neck of only friend.

No Foxy and Bear. Just Bear. Today bad.

Today good again because of new plan: even though hungry, not eat Foxy. Good decision. Foxy not Maury's son, but can still bring Foxy to Bud and Maury. Bring Foxy and show how did not eat thing that ate Maury's son. Even though hungry, even though dying. Plus killed thing that ate Maury's son. So he good. Can come back to Old Ice Kingdom, be with Bud. Miss Bud.

Hope after Maury and Bud see dead Foxy they let eat Foxy. Because hungry. But maybe should not eat friend, even though mad at friend for ruin first plan.

Walk long time, see Old Ice Kingdom on other side of water. Tired because hungry but jump in water anyway. Make halfway across and drop Foxy. Foxy sink. Dive down because need Foxy for plan but can't find. Also can't find top of water. Plan go bad. Feel like Sun go away, even though Sun still there. Tired. Thank Sun for day, even though day not finished. Where is Foxy. Close eyes, even though not in pit. In water. Not good.

◆

Wake up. Having water ride on Dad's back! Best feeling. Favourite thing in world is water ride on Dad's back. Then remember: Dad gone. So, not Dad. Someone else.

Sniff neck fur: Maury. Having water ride on Maury's back. Confused.

Remember swimming to Old Ice Kingdom. Remember dropping Foxy. Was drowning. Means Maury saw drowning, rescue. So Maury not want to kill? Because if want to kill, why rescue? So Maury forgive. This very good.

Holding on to Maury's neck/back, see Old Ice Kingdom shore. See Bud on shore. Maury swimming towards Bud. Bud not scared because not running away. This very good. Maybe get to live in Old Ice Kingdom again where good at killing seal. Where get to be with Bud. Will take Bud for water rides, which is fun for Bud—has good dad like own dad.

As ride to shore, thank Sun, but then remember Foxy. Foxy have son? Not know. Feel bad about Foxy. Best friend now in boundary water.

Go back for Foxy later? Will go back for Foxy later. Will bury Foxy in secret spot, not dig up. Good plan. Thank Sun for plan. Thank Sun for Bud. Bud getting closer. Almost there.

FRANK

Alice sat with her hands folded elegantly on the bar and occasionally sipped her beer. Tillman was late. She thought about going home but she had paid for the room so she ordered another beer. Maybe he would just come. While the bartender was pouring her a new one, a hideous man walked in.

"Thought you'd show up Frank," the bartender said. "How was it today?"

"Evening," Frank said. The ugly man took off his big coat, tucked it somewhere behind the bar then came back around and sat three stools down from Alice. "Was fine. Stout, please."

He looks like a bat, Alice thought. His face was all scrunched up and his hair looked like rat fur. He wore a suit but it wasn't a nice one like the kind Tillman always wore. It was brown but like a dog-food brown.

"Hey Miss," Frank said. He looked right at Alice with his terrible face. I hope this isn't going to be something, she thought.

"Hello," Alice said.

"Here for the convention?"

"No."

"Frank," Frank said extending his hand. Alice had to get up to shake it.

"Alice," she said. She sat back down on her stool as

Frank got up and moved one stool closer. I knew this was going to be something, she thought. If only Tillman was here. And it probably looks like I'm a prostitute because why else would I be sitting here all dressed up with this ugly man. But maybe I'm no treat either which would explain Tillman not showing up. Maybe he walked in the door and saw how I've aged since the last time and walked right back out.

Alice caught her reflection in the mirror behind the bar and realized she was slouching. She sat up straight and regained her elegant pose. Maybe I should put my hair back up, she thought. She'd recently dyed it black and now wondered if she looked like a goth or Cher. Frank was staring at her.

"Your brooch," Frank said. He pointed at the silver owl on Alice's blazer. Tillman had bought it for her. Maybe it was corny of her to wear it but she wanted to so she did. Under the blazer, Alice wore the blue dress from the night she and Tillman had walked around the city until dawn. She carried a pair of flats in her purse in case something like that happened again.

"Yes," she said. "My little owl."

"Can I tell you a story Alice?"

Alice nodded at Frank, looked at her watch and then at Frank.

"When I was a kid there were these woods near my house that I used to play in," Frank said. "One day I was fooling around in there—I was nine at the time— and I saw this little man in a coat through the trees. He was about a foot tall wearing this funny little coat, just walking along. I started to follow him and he didn't seem to notice me.

"The woods stretched pretty far and this tiny man kept walking, slowly. I followed him for maybe twenty minutes. He disappeared in the bushes. It was hard to track him because he was so short. But I kept up. And then when we reached a bit of a clearing I saw that he wasn't a little man in a coat but an owl. It was this owl, just walking through the forest in the middle of the afternoon.

"I stayed on him, though, and eventually the owl walked into this concrete tube that was lying there. It was like a section of a sewer or something. There was some weird junk lying around in that forest. So anyway, I walked up to the tube and looked in. The owl was gone but there was a guy lying in there and he was dead."

"Wow," Alice said. "What happened?"

Before the ugly man could answer, the bartender came over and told Alice there was a phone call for her. She excused herself and went to the other end of the bar where the phone was placed for her to use. She knew that it was Tillman on the other end because no one else knew where she was or what she was doing. But maybe one of the girls from the office found out somehow and she was about to get another lecture.

Of course he didn't show up, they'd say. *Girl, this is wrong. It's so not good for you and it's not good for the poor wife, either. You both deserve better than this.* But they didn't know how it was. They weren't there the night she and Tillman climbed onto her roof and sat there for hours, talking and laughing. They weren't there the first time she slept with Tillman and then cried afterwards because she felt such a deep connection. They were all pretty and had perfect husbands. And it wasn't like any of this was news—she knew it was wrong. They didn't know how it was.

"Hello," Alice said.

"It's me," a voice answered. Alice's spine tingled. It was Tillman. "So guess what? Jane decided to come down with me. This is the first chance I've had to call."

"Can you get away? What do I do?"

"You know I want to be there. Otherwise, you know. But Jane's here at my hotel and I'm in meetings all day. Sorry Alice but you better go home. If she saw you around the city, you know."

"Jesus."

"Just pay for the room and I'll send you some cash when I'm home. Okay, gotta go. I'll try and call soon." A dial tone replaced Tillman's voice but Alice kept holding the phone to her ear. Good thing I got my hair done, she thought. Good thing I spent all that money on my hair and drove all the way to goddamn Windsor and lied to my parents about having the flu and now I'm missing their anniversary dinner with all the family so I can drink with creepy men.

"Okay well thanks for calling. See you tomorrow," Alice said to nobody and hung up the phone. She went back to her stool. She noticed that the two people who were sitting at the table in the back were gone leaving just Frank, the bartender and herself. It was a big room and it was Friday night—both of these facts made the emptiness of the bar feel emptier.

"Sorry about that," Alice said to Frank. The bartender put the phone away and disappeared. "So what happened? After you found the dead guy in the tube?"

"Well, I said 'Hey' a few times to see if the man was sleeping but he didn't wake up. And I just knew he was dead, you know. I could just tell. So I turned around and walked back home, got my dad. He called the constable and I took everyone to the spot. It turned out to be this guy from Detroit who overdosed on pills. Nobody knew what he was doing there, but there he was."

Alice imagined Frank as a little kid but could only picture the bat-faced man in front of her, just smaller.

"And nobody cared about the owl part of it," Frank continued. "Or they didn't believe me. I kept telling them I found the body because I followed the owl but they just thought I was traumatized or something."

"Well yeah," Alice said. "I mean, of course."

"But it was frustrating, you know? I mean, the body was a big deal but people die all the time. It was the owl that was interesting and yet everyone was worried about the little boy who found the corpse. They thought I was scarred by it or something but I wasn't. What had affected me was this owl."

"Because it wasn't just that you found the body," Alice said. "It was that you were, like, meant to find it.

Because this strange owl led you there. That was the amazing thing. You saw something magical."

"Yes!" Frank clapped his hands together and moved one stool closer so that his knees were almost touching Alice's. "It *was* magical."

"People always focus on the wrong things." Alice realized that she probably sounded a little drunk. And she was a little drunk and would be unable to drive back to Toronto now. But it was true what she had said—people always focused on the wrong things. Like the girls at the office who tried to make a charity case out of her when she was fine. When she and Tillman were together the world felt enchanted. Here was this thing that made Alice happy or was at least something exciting in her life but Laura and Kate and Brenda and the others all tried to help her anyway. How after Tillman moved away they tried to set her up with Steve from the office who was a dullard. Which, no offence to poor Steve, was a little insulting.

Alice and Frank talked about their jobs, their parents and the music that played over the bar's speakers. Hotel guests poked their heads into the room as they passed through the lobby but nobody came in. The bartender put a few chairs up in the back.

Alice offered to get the next round but the ugly man said he had to drive home. He walked around behind the bar and put on his coat.

"Come on," Alice said. "There's a couch in my room; you can stay here. Let's have another."

Frank took off his coat and sat back down. Alice felt a hand slide over to her left knee but she didn't slap it away. She just closed her eyes and pictured Tillman—he had beautiful hands.

SKETCH ARTIST, BOXER, PARTY PLANNER, BAKER

On a Greyhound chugging westward, squeezed up against the window by the flabby arm of a sleeping farm boy, Doug Sachs struggled against the darkness of it all. Maybe things weren't so bad, he thought. You've got to see these things as opportunities to grow: *The worse things are, the better they will be.* This would be good. He had helped so many people through their bleakest hours and this was quite an accomplishment—but what of his own battles? He could now see that it was time to turn his healer's gaze inward.

The farm boy was drooping towards him, closer and closer, breathing hot hamburger breath onto his neck. Doug tried pushing him away but the big boy was out cold and wouldn't budge. Wish I could've taken the car, he thought. But again: an opportunity. Lemons/lemonade. Despite the discomfort, taking the bus now meant he had time to prepare for his homecoming.

His mom would inevitably blow things out of proportion: *Carol kicked you out? What did you do? What the hell is wrong with you?* That kind of thing. But there were subtleties and nuances and complications involved and it would take finesse for Doug to unpack and lay out the delicate details of the situation for his mom to see and understand. Which was no problemo. Finesse he could do.

He looked out the window at passing cars; people inside on their own journeys, both geographical and spiritual. He was an hour outside of Ottawa. In another four hours he would change buses in Toronto. It would be five more hours until Sudbury followed by a ten-minute cab ride to his mom's building. He would sleep on her couch for a few days—a week, a month. As long as was needed to come up with a flawless action plan.

In *Sketch Artist, Boxer, Party Planner, Baker*, his self-help book, Doug encouraged the readers to picture their problematic situations as a human body. Try to give everything that's going wrong in your life a face and clothing and expressions, he advised. Gather the confusing, messy, shitty things that keep you awake at night, stitch them together like a Frankenstein's monster and stick a name to it. That way you have a single adversary to overcome, which is encouraging. This is from "Sketch Artist," the first of four steps in Doug's system for tackling dilemmas.

He decided to call the current situation "Norman." Sorry, old Norman! he thought. I'm taking you *out*!

Doug made a list in his head of all the bad things that made up Norman.

1) Carol, his wife, finding a photograph of her older sister, Karen, tucked underneath his side of the mattress.

2) How he, when confronted by Carol about this photograph, confounded her suspicions by failing to produce any kind of explanation, because

a) it was difficult to explain an already tricky situation when suddenly confronted with a picture that he had

    i) been actively hiding from the very person waving it in front of his face and

    ii) stared at, pondered and examined for a rough estimate of five hundred hours.

b) really, there was nothing to say. He was completely obsessed with his wife's sister.

3) How, when Carol left the room to see if the photograph had been plucked from her own family album (it was), he had

a) failed to seize this opportunity to think of something to say that might assuage his wife's reasonable concerns and

b) instead, upon Carol's return to the room, said, "You're not going to tell your sister, are you?"

3) Carol telling her sister about the photograph.

4) The message he then left on Carol's sister's voicemail which amounted to, Hey I know your whole family is kind of rallying against me right now and that we haven't shared but a few sentences in the five years I've known you and that you probably think I'm an unstable creep but what say we take a secret trip to the Dominican together?

5) Carol kicking him out of the house.

And finally, the cherry on top:

6) The hulking mass of the sweaty farm boy in the neighbouring seat closing in, ready to crush him into a sad little diamond.

So that was Norman. The next step in Doug's system would be difficult to complete because a crowded bus was not an optimal space for "Boxer," which involved yelling and punching. The idea was that once one's troubles have been compiled and personified as part of "Sketch Artist," the next step was to express and release one's "surface anger" by verbally and physically abusing an inanimate object representing the figure imagined as part of step one. Carol had sewed together a featureless doll for this purpose, which he had left back at home, but his neck pillow would suffice for now.

The washroom at the back of the bus was Doug's best option for privately abusing his neck pillow—he could mutter insults over the racket of a flushing toilet, throw medium-strength punches out of view of the other passengers and even give little Norman a swirly—but the farm boy had him trapped in his seat for now. Doug took the pillow from his neck and turned towards the window where he could secretly bite into it.

Fuck you, Norman! Doug whispered through clenched teeth. *I hate you and hope you die and rot in hell and get bit by strong teeth like mine every fucking day!* He gnawed on the pillow, making threats and cursing at a volume just below that of the hum of the bus until he began to drool all over the armrest. And that was step two. His surface anger flew out the roof ventilator and he was calm.

By leaning into the window, Doug had caused his seatmate to shift further towards him so that the farm boy's face was now on his shoulder. He tried nudging him off but the big sleeping head was like a concrete slab. Doug wasn't really bothered by this, however. Nope. He had bitten his pillow and was now able to calmly observe the situation for what it was.

Step three, "Party Planner," was about carefully plotting a series of actions which, once performed, would defeat the antagonist imagined in step one of Doug's system. First, you try to visualize the most desirable outcome to your troublesome situation. Then you work backward to figure out a reasonable chain of events that would make this outcome happen. Factor in all limitations, account for variables and use logic to derive a solid, workable plan. Depending on the scope of one's adversary—Norman, for example, was a giant—it often helped to work a small, easily fixed problem into the overall dilemma. That way you can get the ball rolling. The farm boy would be this ball, Norman-wise.

Doug cleared his throat but the boy kept on sleeping. Next, he tried kicking the guy's legs—still nothing. Then he reached into the seat pocket for his water bottle and poured a tiny amount of liquid on his fingers which he then flicked in the farm boy's face. After five or six good flicks, the farm boy awoke and moved back into his own space.

Step one: complete.
Step two: complete.

Doug had zero surface anger because of step two plus peak confidence levels from defeating the farm boy mini-problem which would allow him to plot Norman's demise with a razor-sharp, clear and methodical mind.

Unpinned, Doug reached down between his legs and retrieved his phone from his bag. No calls, no texts. He texted himself the word "hello" to make sure his phone was working. It was. He went into his photo file and brought up the snapshot of the picture of Carol's sister. He wanted a handy digital copy of the tactile photograph on his phone so he could sneak peeks on his way to work, at work, on his way back from work, etc. Carol had come home early from craft night while he was taking the snapshot so he had tucked the original photograph under the mattress before she walked into the room. That night, by chance, Carol decided to change the bedding before Doug had a chance to put the photo back in its album. This was further proof that the whole situation was a good thing: the dumb luck of his wife finding the picture during such a brief window of opportunity was a sign that things needed to change. And change was good. According to Doug's book, "We would all benefit to be more like the bum on the sidewalk, always asking for change."

At first, looking at the photo of Carol's sister was harmless fantasy. Doug would stare at Karen until her tight Disney sweater and sly smile were etched into his brain and then hop in the shower. It was fun to sneak in a little danger while Carol was at work and flirt with taboo. Karen wasn't especially attractive; it was the excitement of playing evil that drew him toward the photo. Soon it became a ritual: once Carol left the house, Doug would pull out the picture and go through scenarios in his head.

1) Karen coming over, teary-eyed and confessing her spicy passion for Doug, whom she would call "Lil' Tamale."

2) Climbing through Karen's apartment window at night with a box of condoms in his teeth and rose petals in his pockets.

3) Carol in a coma—he and Karen acting out a sexy nurse/patient scenario in the adjacent hospital bed.

Eventually, the fact that the photograph was of his wife's sister, or even of a woman, had become irrelevant. What excited Doug about the photograph now was that it was this thing he had stared at for so many hours. If you pay attention to something long enough it takes on a certain aura, Doug realized. There was a religious quality to the photograph now. Carol's sister had the presence of a god or a prophet.

Doug didn't need any gods or prophets, however. He had his system. And as the bus swept past fields and silos and little towns full of people who desperately needed Doug's guidance, he began to plot his triumph over Norman.

After changing buses in Toronto, Doug had a seat to himself and he fell asleep against the window for an hour. When he woke up, a heavy rain was pelting the roof of the bus. For a moment, Doug thought the rain sounds were the withered, knocking hands of Third World children trying to get on the bus and instinctively reached for his bag. When he came to, he pulled out an organic apple oat bar and chewed half.

Things were looking up, Doug thought. "Party Planner" was going extremely well. Not only had he designated a plausible ideal outcome for the whole Norman thing, he had already thought up five possible routes toward reaching it.

The outcome he had come up with was only one compromise away from his first imagined ideal outcome, which was very good. Someone following Doug's guidebook will usually dream up some romantic, blissful outcome and then whittle it down, compromise after compromise, until a more modest and realistic outcome can be decided on. For example, some guy's problem might be that he wants the respect of his father. The guy is unemployed and always asking his dad for money. He'll imagine this perfect outcome where his father respects the hell out of him because he owns a giant, successful company. But then he'll realize he can't own a company because he doesn't know anything about business so he thinks, Okay I'll be some kind of hot shot executive that doesn't need to know all of the business stuff. But then he's not sure if that kind of position exists so he settles for an assistant, then clerk and on down the line until he decides to become the guy who mows the lawn out front of the building. The guy with all the keys on his belt who has to pull dead birds out of the big fountain in the garden. And that's the *plausible* ideal outcome for this guy who wants his dad to be proud of him—to become this maintenance man. Because at least he's working now, even if it's not in an office on the top floor.

Doug's first imagined outcome to the Norman situation, before compromise came into the picture, was that his wife would take him back. Her family would forget everything and the sister would see him on the side—they'd go on secret Dominican trips and give each other leg massages under the table at family dinners. But that would never work. Carol's sister didn't like him and that was that.

To compromise, Doug cut Karen out of the picture and made it simple: the ideal outcome for the Norman problem would be for everything to go back to the way it was. He would be with his wife and her family would forgive and forget. He'd stop obsessing over that damn picture too. A basic "reset" outcome. And this was all within his reach because he had already cooked up five rough plans for achieving this outcome:

1) Claim Ignorance: Gee, Carol, I have no idea what that photo was doing there! I was so

confused by your reaction to finding it I thought I'd just let you run with it for a while. It was clear you needed to work some things out. Hope you're all better now. And someone called up your sister, pretending to be me, and left a weird message? Who would do that? Let's go watch something relaxing on the computer and forget all this madcap nonsense, am I right?

2) Misdirection One: In the background of the photograph, behind Karen in her Disney sweater, stands a man in a tiny swimsuit. Kind of muscular and not bad looking. If Doug were to claim a mysterious attraction to this man and explain the mattress-tuck as a necessary measure while he explored these confusing feelings of possible homosexual leanings there would be many benefits. Carol's lefty family would be too afraid of being seen as insensitive to continue rallying against him; he could pass off the sister-loving stuff as a ploy to hide his embarrassment during this time of self-discovery. He could later explain away the whole thing by claiming a hormonal imbalance due to an overdose of estrogen, because of all the soy he'd been consuming in his shakes at the gym.

3) Misdirection Two: He was hiding the photograph because he was turning Carol's sister Karen into a knight. He had planned on taking

pictures of all their friends and family out of the album—one by one, so Carol wouldn't notice—so as to scan the faces and make a chess set for Carol's birthday. She was to be the Queen and he the King. The other family members would be pieces on the back row and their acquaintances would be pawns. He didn't want to ruin the surprise and so he let his wife jump to conclusions while he finished off the set. Only problem: he would actually have to make this chess set using whatever pictures he could find online since he didn't have access to the photo album. But not really a problem because he could do it.

4) Shadow Doug: It wasn't me, Carol! I just plain wasn't myself for a minute there. Because of work stress or allergies or a hormonal imbalance due to all the soy.

5) Hidden Camera Hoax: He could make a video where he would place the photograph in the mattress, turn to the camera, say "Shhh" and leave the room. Then an actress who resembles his wife but whose face couldn't really be seen because of the camera angle would come into the shot and re-enact finding the photo. Then Doug would come back into the room and he and the actress would go through the whole fight (as best as he could remember and

choreograph). He would have to be wearing the same clothes he wore at the time. When the fake Carol left the room, he would come back in and hold up a sign saying "Gotcha!" and give a big thumbs-up. He would show the video to Carol and she would think the whole thing was a crazy prank that went haywire.

All Doug had to do now was pick a plan and follow through with it. That was called "Baker," the following-through step. If a plan was solid, one only had to stick to it and the plausible ideal outcome would become a reality. Like a baker—just follow the recipe.

The sky was full of dark clouds and the rain made an enormous racket as it dinged the roof of the bus but Doug had the advantage of being an optimist. The clouds and the rain were not for him but the gloom spelled out impending disaster for Norman. He could see Norman quivering at the sight of nature gathering together and conspiring against him under Doug's supervision. Norman wasn't a giant at all; he was just fat. He was that big fat farm boy. Greasy and foul and fat and easily dominated by Doug. All he had to do was flick his fingers and Norman would back off.

Doug fell asleep against the window again but woke up a minute later clutching his bag. He was sweating through his shirt. *The worse things are, the better they will be*, he reminded himself.

THIS DEER WON'T LOOK BOTH WAYS

That sign you sometimes pass on the highway with the painted silhouette of the deer? That's me. I won't look both ways. It's true, I won't. I'll just walk right into the road, suddenly, while it's dark. My friends will too, so be warned. Not that it matters—you'll hit us anyway. We *want* to get hit.

I'm not stupid. I can hear a car coming from miles away and I've been run down nine times since Christmas. Obviously, I try to avoid full-on collisions; I don't want to die. Just a good hit to the hindquarters, something that will throw me into the culvert. One time I got smacked in the face with a side-view mirror. God that was good.

My cousin Aaron? He likes to watch from the bushes while we get struck. That's his thrill. Not me—I crave that rush you can only get when four thousand pounds of metal knock you into a spin, that wild screech of rubber on pavement, the sudden panic that this might be the one that finally cripples you for life. I dream about this every night.

The thing I really fantasize about is that one night a driver will stop and reverse slowly over my tail. And then maybe they get out and slam one of my legs in the car door. Oh god. Maybe they tie me up like they're going to mount me on the roof rack but instead they just douse me in windshield washer fluid. Yes.

Because what else is there for me and my friends? Do you know what we do all day? Picture one of those deer-hunting arcade games they have in sports bars with the plastic guns: you wander around a boring forest, looking at trees or at nothing until you see a stag—and then you shoot it. Kind of entertaining, right? Now imagine that instead of shooting the deer, you just look at it for a second, nod and then continue wandering around until you see another one. And then you nod again. That's it. That's my life. I just want to feel something other than the slow digestion of the cud I chew. So we go out at night and look for release in a pair of headlights.

See this scar on my back? A few months ago I ran out in front of this pickup and the guy who came to check on me dropped a lit cigar on the side of the road about ten feet from where I lay bleeding. I knew I had to seize this golden opportunity and I wiggled my way over to it, salivating. The driver jumped back into his truck, probably thinking I was rabid or something but I wiggled my way over and rolled onto the stogie. Jesus. It was like a blinding white light from heaven. Smoke rose in the retreating lights of the pickup and the smell was like grilled venison. My cousin Aaron was in the bushes the whole time watching and chewing on his foreleg. People see these bald patches on our legs and think it's because of ticks or something, but no. We do this to ourselves because we *can*.

You know what those signs along the highway should say? *This Deer Won't Mind If You Swerve into Him.*

Or: *This Deer Would Be Delighted If You Were to Pull Over, Grab Him by the Antlers and Bash His Head into the Hood of Your Car Until He Loses Consciousness.*

Or, wait: *This Deer Wants You to Run Over His Hind Legs So He Can't Move Away, Watch Him Writhe There in the Middle of the Road While You Drink a Fifth of Scotch and Then Piss Right on His Face While His Pervert Cousin Watches from the Bushes and Feverishly Bites into His Own Leg Thus Humiliating the Struck Deer Until He Finally Reaches the Carrot That Has Been Dangling in Front of Him His Entire Adult Life as He Experiences Pure, Unbridled Ecstasy.*

But, whatever. The current signage is better than the usual bland, DEER CROSSING. And I understand if you'd rather obey the warning and drive with caution because hitting us is a danger to you guys too. You've got sports bars, malls and water parks—things to really live for. Just promise me you won't feel bad if you happen to run us down. You'll notice, as the headlights of your vehicle bear down on me, that this deer won't look both ways. This deer will look directly into your own eyes. This is not fear; this is not a plea to your humanity. I am looking into the eyes of my master. Dominate me. Humble me with your awesome power, driver. Oh yes.

THE GIRL WHO SMELLED OF SARSAPARILLA

t began during a power outage. The TV went out one Sunday night and my dad decided to tell us a story to pick up the slack. Mom lit candles. My sister Kat and I sat on the rug. I was ten years old, my sister eleven.

Dad improvised the whole thing. It was a Western tale about a nameless girl who had her own six-shooter. She rode a horse called Poncho and went on adventures. Dad said she drank twenty bottles of sarsaparilla a day and people could smell it on her—you'd know right away when she walked into the room, he said. Some of the strangers she'd run into on the trail would laugh at her. Who was this strange little cowgirl? Shouldn't she be with her dolls? But those who knew her by reputation would let her pass wordlessly, frightened by what she might do if they upset her in any way. The girl didn't play with dolls—she played with bullets, throwing knives and broken sarsaparilla bottles.

Kat and I were sold. When the TV and lights came back on we begged our father to turn everything off again and continue his tale. He did. After that, Sunday evenings were story night when Dad would continue the serialization of "The Girl Who Smelled of Sarsaparilla." We loved hearing of the girl's adventures on the range. She was always getting into trouble. Dad would put his brave protagonist into horrifying situations—like when she fell into a snakepit, or the firepit, or the one pit that had snakes *and* fire and the snakes were somehow immune to the fire—but he'd always pull her out of there before Kat and I got too nervous. Dad would pace around the room while he talked. He did voices and made gestures. When the girl spit, Dad would spit too—right onto the carpet.

A few months later—mid-February, I think—Dad got laid off. The auto plant he worked for shut down and he found he had a lot of free time. In the mornings, he'd check the paper for jobs but come afternoon he occupied himself with research. He wanted to make the stories he told us better, more accurate, he said. He wanted to nail down all the historical details of the American Old West so he'd walk down to the library and come home with an armload of books. He'd plunk them down on the kitchen table and sit there in his pajama bottoms, unshaven, flipping pages and jotting notes until midnight or later. His bathrobe would be open, his gut spilled out over his lap. Sometimes he'd stay up until morning.

The stories changed after that. Dad concerned himself less and less with narrative. It became more about the details, the historical details he'd found in his books. One Sunday, Dad taped a nineteenth-century map of the American states and territories to the wall and sat us down in front of it for story time. He'd copied it from one of his books. It was covered with his own little sketches and notations, which he explained.

"Now this road here was originally a postal route

but was taken over by the town of Challis when it sprang up in 1850," he'd say. "But the interesting thing is that in 1866, Challis burned down and the road fell into disrepair. It was forgotten for decades until a new town—Saint Rose, I think—came into being. They fixed it up and now it's part of the Texas highway system. You can still drive down that route, kids."

Where was the girl? Kat and I wondered. *What happened to the adventures?* But we couldn't say anything. The job market was scarce at the time and these American history lectures were all he cared about. I began to dread Sunday evenings.

For a month or so, all his stories began with the girl heading off to the schoolhouse and then Dad would spend a few hours describing the history lessons she was taught that day. It didn't make sense. If the girl lived in the Old West, why would her teacher spend the entire class going on about what it was like living in the Old West? Couldn't the students just look out the window?

Dad finally found work. He had to take a counter job at Wendy's. It wasn't his first choice, but it was a paycheque. He shaved for the first time since losing his job and decided to leave a moustache. Mom said he looked like a peeping tom but Dad kept it. He wanted a new look, a fresh start. He continued to serialize "The Girl Who Smelled of Sarsaparilla" on Sunday nights but thankfully he dropped the historical stuff. He got back to the story. During her wanderings, the girl stopped in the town of Grayhorse and found work as a barmaid in the local saloon. She was only ten years old but the other barmaids were even younger—seven, six years old. They were tykes with no worldly knowledge, never having travelled the range, but they had seniority since they'd been working at the saloon for longer. "Hurry up with them sours, slowpoke," the precocious little brats would say. "Better grab the mop, lazy bones. Old Wesley done chucked up again."

And the saloon's patrons—Dad could spend a whole evening describing the saloon's patrons and their exploits. "One night," he'd say, "this big butterball of a man came rolling into the girl's saloon. He ordered five rabbit stews, all to himself. Ate them right there in the restaurant. Left a big mess too. The girl had to stand there and watch from behind the bar. She couldn't look away on account of she couldn't believe it. And then this big boy finishes his five stews, walks back up and demands another two!"

Our hero had stopped riding Poncho around and ceased to find herself in duels. No more dangerous pits. Nothing fun, just work stories, and Kat and I saw right through his disguise. The saloon's "trot-through" was really the drive-thru, the oversized pink stetson the girl was made to wear stood for the ball cap and headset Dad was so embarrassed of and the outlaws pushing moonshine by the stables were clearly the teenagers who sold OxyContin in the parking lot. Dad's imagination only stretched so far, I suppose.

It was around this time that my parents started getting into huge fights. I guess Mom felt like Dad resented her for making more money than he did. She worked at the bank. In turn, Dad felt like Mom resented *him* for making less money than *she* did. They'd have complicated arguments and Mom would drive off to meet her friends in a huff leaving Dad with us. He'd tell his Western tales on these nights, even if it wasn't a Sunday.

Soon, Poncho the horse came to represent our mother in Dad's stories. When the girl finished her saloon shifts she'd come outside to find Poncho untied from the hitching post and nowhere to be seen. Poncho left vague notes for the girl written in the dirt with her hoof: *Horsey night, don't wait up*, or *Off horsin' around, Myra got a new salt lick*. Sometimes Poncho would come into the saloon with her horse friends—at this point Dad was happy to explore any ridiculous idea that popped into his head—and pretend not to know the girl. Poncho would hide in a booth near the back muttering that they never should've come there; if one of the other horses recognized the girl behind the bar, Poncho would just change the subject. Dad's tales were getting tense, told with a serious expression that made me and my sister extremely uncomfortable. Often we'd pretend to fall asleep so Dad would have to take us up to bed, though there were times he wouldn't acknowledge our fake snores; times he would get so caught up he wouldn't have noticed if we left the room.

That summer things took a turn for the worse. Mom left. We weren't aware of this at the time but later learned that Mom had an affair and Dad found out.

Mom moved into her own apartment and we stayed in the house with Dad. The saga of "The Girl Who Smelled of Sarsaparilla" became a nightly event. And things got dark.

"One morning," Dad said, staring into his beer glass, "the girl didn't feel like going into the saloon. So she didn't. She stayed in bed. She stayed in bed and she drank sarsaparillas like she always did except they tasted like puddle water and bad breath. She drank them anyway. And she didn't sleep, even though she was in bed. She just lay there and wondered what Poncho was doing. Maybe Poncho was dead. How would she know? She looked up at the ceiling and saw shapes and all the shapes looked like Poncho trampling little girls. She put the covers over her head and cried. She only got up to use the latrine, and once she was done, she'd get right back into bed. If only I could do this every day, she'd think. But some days she *had* to go to the saloon and it was hard to see why exactly, but she did. She'd rather just stay in bed and look at the terrible shapes in the ceiling because even though those days were no good, they were better than the days she went to the saloon. Christ."

He told us these stories before bed and then Kat and I would go and have nightmares. We begged our father to stop, to get back to the adventures with Poncho, but he wouldn't listen. He had a glaze over his eyes. It was like he couldn't hear anything beyond his own gloomy thoughts.

By the end of the summer, Dad had lost his job

at Wendy's. He'd skipped out on too many shifts and that was it. Mom moved in with Steve, the man she'd been having the affair with, and then Dad got bit by a baby racoon while he was cleaning out the garage. "The Girl Who Smelled of Sarsaparilla" stopped lying around in bed, however; Dad had her head out onto the range again. The stories became increasingly more violent, with the girl shooting and stabbing her way through the Old West. If anyone looked at her funny, she'd pluck out their eyeballs and throw them into a creek. If a beggar asked for scraps, she'd force-feed him dirt until he choked. She'd burn herself with cigars to pass the time and put rocks in her shoes for reasons that were left unexplained. And then she met Reverend Hoss.

Hoss was a doomsday preacher who travelled from town to town, setting up a crate on the main drag and climbing up to tell passersby about the coming apocalypse. The girl would follow him around and help the reverend carry his crate until Dad eventually stopped mentioning the girl altogether. He just went on about Hoss and recreated his ominous speeches.

"The frontier is a black abyss," Dad would say in a deep drawl, arms gesturing wildly above his head. "As civilization creeps westward, we are walking right into the great jaws of Lucifer. And there's no turning back. We're on a slope and you'd better believe we're sliding. No man can escape this slide. I'm talking brimstone. I'm talking heavy chains and black smoke and sharp rocks. I'm talking flames so hot it's beyond our comprehension. Think of that: *beyond comprehension.* These are end days, people."

For weeks, our father was obsessed with hell. He'd describe the underworld over dinner using his Hoss voice. It was horrifying, of course, but the most disturbing thing was that the details didn't come from intense research, as with his earlier Old West tales— they came from his imagination. He'd go on about fountains of blood, red clouds that rained children's shoes and sentient rivers that cried out in pain through the night. Kat and I didn't sleep much that summer.

Word of Dad's behaviour made it to Mom and she was able to convince him to seek therapy. He'd go in for weekly sessions and they put him on antidepressants and tranquilizers. He slept a lot. He was calm. Kat and I moved in with our mother and Steve so Dad could rest but we'd visit on weekends. He'd continue the tale of "The Girl Who Smelled of Sarsaparilla" on Sundays before Mom would pick us up. The tone of the stories changed again.

"The girl got on her horsey," Dad would say. "The horsey was named Poncho. They were friends. They went on an adventure. They rode to a canyon. They found nice flowers and smelled the flowers. Then they were tired. They had naps in the flowers. It was a good adventure." That sort of thing.

It took time but our father made it through this difficult period. The therapy sessions were productive and after about a year he weaned himself off the medication. He found a job at a call centre and worked his way up to a management position. He met a woman there whom he eventually married. Kat and I still saw him on weekends but he discontinued the story of the girl. My sister and I were fine with this decision.

Dad didn't speak of the Old West until much later when I was in college. I was having a rough time—the girl I was seeing left me for a mutual friend, my grades were slipping and I injured my back falling into a ditch while drunk. Dad came to visit me in my dorm. He was sitting by my bed, listening to my complaints and then he interrupted me. He started back in on the girl as if a decade hadn't passed since the previous chapter.

"Poncho was having a bad day and so the girl boxed his ears and looked right into his eyes," Dad said. I guess Poncho was *me* now. "And she told him to quit bellyaching because there was sarsaparilla to drink and adventures to have and goddammit if there wasn't but one cloud in that big blue sky."

"Easy for her to say," I said.

"No," Dad said. "Not easy."

DEROSA

For the second year in a row, Ted Cohen spent his birthday in a room at the Cedars–Sinai Medical Center. The previous year, his wife was in the bed. Now it was a man named DeRosa.

"So who's gonna sing me the birthday song?" Ted said.

DeRosa's cardiac monitor beeped.

"Wake up and sing for me. Don't be rude, DeRosa."

The patient wore what looked like a white motorcycle helmet of bandages covering the wound Ted had given him the week prior when he'd brained DeRosa with a landscape painting. If you leaned in close, Ted discovered, the helmet smelled like an armpit. The rest of the room smelled like lemons.

DeRosa didn't live in South Roberston or even Los Angeles. He came from Texas, a police officer had told Ted. They couldn't get a hold of the patient's family so it was just Ted there during visiting hours. He'd been there every day that week.

A nurse walked in. She had beautiful blonde curls and heavy bags under her eyes. She was new, hired within the past year. Before Ted's wife died he basically lived at Cedars–Sinai. For two months, he watched poor Annie shrivel and fade. And here he was again, freshly seventy-two, and on a first-name basis with almost everyone who worked in Intensive Care. He watched the new girl change DeRosa's IV drip.

"Hello there," Ted said. "What's your name?"

The nurse seemed deeply focused on the drip.

"Yes, his condition is stable," she said, eventually. "So that's good. We'll have to stay positive, right? I'll be just outside if you need me."

She left the room and Ted shook a fist.

"You hear that, DeRosa?"

DeRosa's monitor beeped.

"And you're no better. Why don't you wake up and say something already? Wake up, DeRosa. I've got words for you." He needed the man to wake up. He had so many questions: Who *are* you? Why did you break in to my house? What do you want from me that you can't get back in Texas?

When the coma spell broke, Ted would be there, waiting. He wasn't interested in pressing charges; he wanted to deal with DeRosa himself. Give the schmuck a lecture, show him who's boss and get some answers.

Ted pulled a Pall Mall from his pack and stood up.

"I'm just stepping outside. When I come back, I expect your little nap to be over. I've got words for you, DeRosa."

DeRosa's monitor beeped.

Correspondence between Ernesto DeRosa (Dispatcher, Lake Jackson Taxi) and Ted Cohen (Executive Producer, F·R·I·E·N·D·S), July 2003

Dear Ted Cohen,

I am writing to you now regarding the unfortunate decision to stop the production of new *Friends* episodes following the upcoming tenth season. I realize this decision may not be entirely, or perhaps at all, yours but I also know that as a writer and an executive producer you must wield considerable clout. Use it!

The official NBC press release concerning this decision states that those involved in the creation of *Friends* feel the series has "run its course" and that the "story must conclude," etc. Excuse me? This is ridiculous. *Friends* is the greatest sitcom or even show of all time and the gang will never run out of fun experiences to share. Do you know *Coronation Street*, the British soap? It's not anywhere near as strong as *Friends* but has been running for over forty years now and I feel that *Friends* can and should continue for forty more years, or even longer, or at least until a significant portion of the lead actors die.

Please add this letter to the mountain of likeminded letters I hope you are receiving right now and take a good, long look at that mountain. Look at that mountain and use your clout. It's not too late to reconsider.

Sincerely,
Ernesto DeRosa

◆

Dear Fan,

Thank you so much for your thoughtful letter. We at NBC recognize that the quality programming we work hard to bring you would not exist without your support. As a token of our appreciation we have included a complimentary packet of postcards highlighting NBC's exciting new fall lineup.

Yours,
Stephanie Lyons, Audience Outreach
NBC Studios, 30 Rockefeller Plaza, New York, NY

◆

Dear Ted Cohen,

Thanks for your speedy reply, although this reply came from some Stephanie Lyons and not you, whom I addressed the letter to. Why is this Stephanie reading and replying to a letter that I sent to you? Anyway, I'm sure you are buried in fan mail pleading for the continuation of *Friends* right now but I feel like I wasn't specific enough with my last one and that there are some things you should know. Like I didn't really communicate how much *Friends* means to me.

It means a great deal, Ted. I began watching your program with my family during Season Three. We'd gather around the TV set every Thursday night and I'd make popcorn. My wife Susan and I sat on either ends of the sofa with our son Gabe between us. We'd turn down the lights and really get into the episode and had this rule where we could only talk during ads. Susan's favourite was Phoebe because she liked her songs. I'm a Joey man. My son likes Chandler and his endless quips—we all laughed at Chandler together. We caught up on reruns and kept our Thursday night tradition alive until Susan left me during Season Six. I was devastated but Gabe and I continued with Thursday night *Friends* until Season Seven, when I lost custody of Gabe. I was devastated again.

The point, Ted, is that I kept watching every Thursday night by myself and I'll do the same with Season Ten and hopefully the seasons to follow. I have Seasons One through Five on DVD and I watch them regularly. I watch reruns when they come on too. Sometimes I'll turn on the TV halfway through a gem from Season Four, watch it and then pull out the DVD and watch the beginning of that same episode. But it's so good I keep going and watch the second half all over again and then watch the next episode too.

And when I watch *Friends* I'm not just watching because it's my favourite show and sometimes I feel like the friends on *Friends* are my best friends. I'm also watching because it reminds me of the golden days when my family was a family and we always had Thursday nights to look forward to together. Sometimes I'll even turn to offer Gabe popcorn, realize he's not there and then I'll cry. I'll cry and wipe my eyes with my hands which have butter from the popcorn all over them and then I get butter in my eyes and cry even more because of the physical pain on top of the mental pain. When I finally stop, I'll look up and there's Chandler proposing to Monica and the tears will come again, then the butter and more weeping.

As you can see, *Friends* is all tangled up with my deepest emotions and if you kill *Friends*, in a way you're killing me. My stress levels are already high and if they climb higher because of the end of Friends, I don't know what I'll do. I feel like I have to do something to stop this so I'm writing you this letter but I don't know if that's enough. I hope you're listening.

Friends is the only good thing in my life. Except for my wife and son, but they aren't really in my life anymore so perhaps they don't count. Please, Ted.

Sincerely,
Ernesto DeRosa

◆

Dear Fan,
Thank you so much for your thoughtful letter. We at NBC recognize that the quality programming we work hard to bring you would not exist without your support. As a token of our appreciation, we have included a complimentary packet of postcards highlighting NBC's exciting new fall lineup.

Yours,
Stephanie Lyons, Audience Outreach
NBC Studios, 30 Rockefeller Plaza, New York, NY

◆

I'll just do it, Ted Cohen thought. I'll reach over, pry his lips open with my fingers and sneak a peek.

He stood up, walked to the doorway and looked down the hallway. Empty. He went over to DeRosa. Nothing had changed—still a sad lump on a hospital bed. A sad, mysterious lump the nurses had to shift every three hours to prevent bedsores from forming. Ted wiped his hands on his pants and then touched DeRosa's face. It was cold but the cardiac monitor kept beeping so he had to be alive. Ted pulled up DeRosa's top lip. There it was along the upper row of teeth. A gap, just as he'd expected.

A few weeks earlier, Ted found a tooth while vacuuming his living room carpet. He almost sucked it into the Hoover but swerved just in time.

"Well, look at you," Ted said, stooping.

He palmed the tooth and gave it a squint. He could tell it had come from a human mouth. Off-white enamel, a spot of blood on the roots. He held it under his nose—no real smell. A regular American tooth.

Ted stuck a finger in his mouth and prodded. Wasn't his. He had all his teeth, which was a source of pride at his age. He considered that the tooth may have belonged to Annie. She had been gone a year now, though, and he always kept up with the cleaning. He would've found it earlier if it were Annie's.

Had there been any visitors? Ted wondered. He couldn't remember. Annie was the social one. A few days earlier he'd bought a box of cookies from a Girl Guide; maybe she had ripped out a loose incisor and hucked it across the room while he was retrieving his wallet. Hard to come up with a motive to go along with that theory, though. Most likely he had stepped on it outside. In the parking lot at the bank, perhaps. It got stuck in the treads of his shoe and he tracked it inside. There, solved. He put the tooth in a cup and put the cup on top of the fridge. He finished vacuuming the living room.

The next day, when Ted began to make toast he noticed that a chunk of the bread loaf was missing. There should have been three-quarters instead of half. Guess I ate it, he thought. He made his toast. He watched golf on TV, took a nap, drove to the 7-Eleven and bought a case of Dr. Pepper. He ate a ham sandwich for dinner. He watched more golf, drank two Dr. Peppers and went to bed. An ordinary Ted Cohen evening.

In the middle of the night, Ted awoke with a painfully full bladder. He flicked on the bedside lamp and sat up but before he could put on his slippers he heard a noise coming from down the hall. It sounded like a drawer shutting—or maybe a cereal box falling from the kitchen counter. Ted sat still, listening, and gripped his blanket. The house was silent.

Oh Christ, he thought. The tooth, the missing bread. Someone's been breaking in, some junkie, and he's been eating my bread and using my stove to get high. And he's in my house right now. Some lunatic hophead is in my house, whacked out of her mind, or *minds*—could be an entire gang. A whole platoon of fearless, gap-toothed junkies crouching in my kitchen and if I don't go to the bathroom this minute, there's going to be laundry to do.

Ted stepped out of bed and into his slippers. He moved towards the hallway carefully, listening for a break in the silence. Had to be the garbage shifting, he thought. Sometimes a plastic muffin container or Styrofoam tray that's been crushed will suddenly pop back into place. Or it could have been a mouse or even a dream.

Inside the bathroom, he locked the door and sat down on the toilet. His urine hit the water like a laser beam. Over the gurgle in the bowl, Ted thought he heard another noise—another drawer shutting or a knock but he couldn't stop the force of his stream. Oh Jesus Christ, he thought. If only poor, dear Annie were here. She always kept his paranoia in check like when he suspected the neighbours were skinheads or when he thought a rash on his chest meant lung cancer. "Mr. Vogel is bald," Annie had said, "not an anti-Semite." It's just a rash, an infected hair follicle, not a tumour. She was the rational one and now she was gone and his imagination was free to run amok. There was nobody to hear his latest delusions and identify them as such.

Ted flushed and listened: the house was quiet again. He pulled up his pants, unlocked the door and moved slowly down the hall. He hit the kitchen light switch and scanned the room—everything was as it should be. No junkies, no gang. He checked the front door. Locked. He walked around the living room, inspecting under the couch and behind the TV. No dirty needles, no more teeth. He decided to return to his bed but as he made his way past the area where he had found the tooth, something soaked through the bottom of his slippers. There was a small dark patch on the carpet beneath his feet. Ted kicked off his right slipper and gave it a sniff—Dr. Pepper. He hadn't spilled any soda himself because he had opened, emptied and left his cans over by the couch. Someone was there. Someone was in his house, drinking his pop, spilling it and hiding in the shadows.

He searched the room for a weapon. A kitchen knife would be threatening, Ted thought, but you'd have to get in close to use it. The curtain rod was too flimsy. If only he hadn't sold his golf clubs. He'd find something, then coax the intruder from his hiding place and give her hell. He had to. If he called the police, it'd take too long. If he ran away, the intruder might escape. This was Ted's show and he had a plan. He pulled one of Annie's watercolours off the wall—the beach scene in the heavy oak frame. A shame, but his best bet. He leaned it against the wall by the front door like a sword.

Ted walked into the kitchen, picked up the phone, punched in several zeros and covered the earpiece with his hand.

"Hey, Jim?" he said, loudly. "Sorry I'm so late, I accidentally fell asleep. Yeah. I'll be there as soon as I can. I'm leaving right now. I owe you one. Yeah, I'll come in for my next shift early so you can take off or something. Anyway, I'm leaving *right now* so just hold on. Okay, bye."

He walked back to the front entrance, picked up the painting and opened the door. He took a few steps in place but didn't go outside. He closed the door. He waited.

Ted remained still, breathing slowly through his nose. He listened. He watched the kitchen before him. A minute passed. Another minute passed and then the cupboard beneath the sink opened up. One leg emerged and then the other. A soda can rolled out from inside the cupboard and onto the floor. Ted lifted Annie's beach scene above his head.

Correspondence between Ernesto DeRosa (Dispatcher, Lake Jackson Taxi) and Ted Cohen (Executive Producer, F·R·I·E·N·D·S), July–August 2003

Dear Ted Cohen,

Okay, so Stephanie? If you are reading this, please don't send me any more postcards and just pass this back to Ted Cohen. This letter has been addressed to and should be read and replied to by Ted Cohen and only Ted Cohen.

Alright, so Ted. I feel like I was still a little vague with my last letter regarding who I am and why *Friends* is so important to me. Perhaps you are wondering why my wife left me or why I lost custody of Gabe. Perhaps you're thinking, "Who cares what that Ernesto thinks, he can't even keep his family together." Or, "That Ernesto thinks he has this special pain because his family has fallen apart? What about all the other hundreds of people in the same situation? Who does he think he is, that Ernesto?" But listen: I am your audience. I am the average American. I have problems and I do the best I can. And if I'm but one voice amongst thousands then that shows you the impact of *Friends*. Hear my story and you hear the story of our great country.

What happened with my wife is that she left me for a man she worked with named Levon. But don't sympathize with me too much because in retrospect it was a little bit my fault. See, years ago, when Season Five of *Friends* was airing, Susan and I were out for dinner at an Italian restaurant here in Lake Jackson called Paul's, owned by Susan's friend Paul. It was our anniversary and we had risotto and white wine. I had more white wine than I did risotto and it was December and icy and after dinner I slipped in the parking lot. My spine connected with the curb and I had to wear a back brace all winter.

I missed two weeks of work and wages. And during that "vacation" I happened to see an ad for one of those accident lawyers on TV. I called him up and he said I had a case. Susan pleaded with me, said not to sue, said that it was her friend Paul I'd be hurting—our friend Paul. I said that I was the one hurting, said look at this awful brace. Because I'm the kind of guy who fights for what is right, for what I'm owed. Just like I'm fighting for my family and just like I'm fighting for the continuation of *Friends*.

We argued. I wouldn't listen and Susan grew cold. We still watched *Friends* together and she helped me with my brace but she looked at me differently after that. Like I was some kind of monster—not because I was crippled but because I was suing her friend Paul. I kept on with the lawsuit, I gave it my all and I won. Ended up with fifty thousand dollars after my lawyer's fees. Paul had to shut down his death trap. I tried to rub my new fortune in my wife's face but she didn't want anything to do with the money. I'd buy her gifts and she'd throw them in the yard.

By that time, I had developed a small dependency on the painkillers I was taking for my back. I needed them though. I was in agony. Sometimes I'd wash the pills down with white wine which may have caused some unnecessary outbursts of anger. I was going through a lot, you must understand. Hard times. Susan began her affair with Levon. She sneaked around with him for months. I had no idea. When she finally told me what had been going on and that she was moving in with this other man—at this point Season Six was on the air—I couldn't believe it. I had Gabe with me though and I had *Friends*. I put the money from the lawsuit in a special account for Gabe's college fund. We watched *Friends* on Thursday nights before Susan and Levon would take him for the weekend.

Then during Season Six, Gabe fell off my roof. I still don't know what he was doing up there. At this point in my life, I was in a lot of pain and had upped my dosage of back medicine. I was drinking a lot of wine too, because it reminded me of romantic nights with Susan. Sometimes I'd swallow enough wine and pills that I'd pass out for an entire afternoon. I'd pass out in my recliner in front of the *Friends* Season Two DVD menu screen, a snippet of the theme song playing over and over, which is exactly how the neighbour found me the day Gabe fell off the roof.

I woke up in the hospital and they pumped my stomach. I was fine. The nurses told me that Gabe was on another floor, that he had fallen and hit his head. He was doing well but apparently there had been a scare. I guess, technically, he had died for about a minute on the way to the hospital.

Things moved rather quickly and soon Gabe moved in with Susan and Levon. I could still visit Gabe but there were all of these terms. I had to book two weeks in advance, I had to take a Breathalyzer test and a social worker had to be present. The hardest thing of all, though, was the calls from Gabe. He'd secretly phone me up late at night and talk about his brief death. He said he had been to heaven on the day of the accident, quite literally—that while his heart was stopped momentarily in the back of that ambulance, he had floated up and out of his body and met with God. He'd go on about how beautiful heaven was and how there were no bad feelings, only good feelings. He said he could have any toy he wanted, or any dessert, like he could just snap his fingers and whatever he desired would appear but that he didn't need to snap his fingers because just being in heaven was enough. You didn't need toys or cake because sitting still and thinking about the fact that you were in heaven was pure bliss.

He said he wanted to die. He said he wanted me to kill him so he could go back to heaven because Mom said he wouldn't go to heaven if he killed himself—instead he'd go to hell. So here I was, alone, struggling with back pain and terrible hangovers with no one to comfort me and listening to my nine-year-old beg me to come over and suffocate him with his Dallas Cowboys pillow. Poor, young Gabe. Susan put him in therapy. He's doing better now. He won't back down from the idea that he's been to heaven but he's agreed that he needs to live out his existence on Earth before he can return to the afterlife. You can see it in his eyes, though. He's just waiting. My poor son.

This is what I'm up against. I had a perfect life with a loving partner and a son who laughed at Chandler with me and now I have nothing. I have *Friends*, yes, but maybe not for long. So should I give up? Should I throw in the towel, NBC-style, and just forget about Susan and Gabe and the Thursday nights we shared together? Did our little sitcom "run its course" by Season Five, before the lawsuit and Levon and Gabe's accident messed everything up? No. I will never give up. I'll reunite my family, whatever it takes. I'm trying to drink less and ease up on the back pills. I can do it. And so can you.

Let's save *Friends*, Ted. In a dark, scary world we

need all the light we can get and *Friends* shines brilliantly. Let it shine, Ted. Let the light of it beam down on all of us.

Sincerely,
Ernesto DeRosa

◆

Dear Fan,

Thank you so much for your thoughtful letter. We at NBC recognize that the quality programming we work hard to bring you would not exist without your support. As a token of our appreciation, we have included a complimentary packet of postcards highlighting NBC's exciting new fall lineup.

Yours,
Stephanie Lyons, Audience Outreach
NBC Studios, 30 Rockefeller Plaza, New York, NY

◆

Dear Ted Cohen/Stephanie,

I warned you Stephanie. I want to talk to Ted. Tell Ted that I need to talk to him. I need him to hear what I have to say. Let's say, hypothetically, that Ted is ignoring my heartfelt letters. That I make myself vulnerable in writing these letters but still he ignores them. And, hypothetically, let's say I wanted to talk to him so much that I hired a private detective whom I met through the lawyer who handled my Paul's lawsuit. Let's say I gave this detective some of Gabe's college fund and that he found Ted's address in Los Angeles. Let's say I'm confused why the NBC website would tell people to write its producers in New York if they actually live on the west coast—let's say I'm sick of playing games. Let's say I have enough college funds and back pills to get me to Ted's house. Let's say I have the information, money and time to get me to the real Casa de Cohen where we can talk about these issues of great importance face to face. Let's say I'm sick of postcards and I need Ted Cohen to listen. Really listen.

So tell Ted that I hope he reads my letters and writes me back ASAP because that would be a whole lot easier than having to drive across three states and spend more of Gabe's college money to see Ted in person. Tell him I'm waiting. And if he's too busy to write back, you can tell him I'm coming for him. Hypothetically.

Sincerely,
Ernesto DeRosa

◆

Dear Fan,

Thank you so much for your thoughtful letter. We at NBC recognize that the quality programming we work hard to bring you would not exist without your support.

As a token of our appreciation, we have included a complimentary packet of postcards highlighting NBC's exciting new fall lineup.

Yours,

Stephanie Lyons, Audience Outreach

NBC Studios, 30 Rockefeller Plaza, New York, NY

◆

It began to rain and Ted needed a Pall Mall so he took DeRosa's jean jacket from the other chair. It fit him perfectly. He went outside.

It had been a month now and the coma was still going strong. Ted was determined, however, to ride this thing out with the stubborn Texan. I'm not giving up, he thought, and DeRosa's not giving up either. He's going to wake up and get what's coming, the schmuck. I'm getting my answers. That's just how it's going to be.

Outside, Ted stood under a palm tree and lit up. He put his lighter into DeRosa's jacket pocket and noticed there was something else in there. He pulled out a thick stack of postcards.

Scrubs, *American Dreams*, *Miss Match*, *F.R.I.E.N.D.S.*, etc. They were TV-show ads.

Then he noticed the back of the postcards which were covered in a tiny, neat handwriting. It looked like a script. The cards were numbered in the bottom right-hand corner. Ted shuffled them into order and began to read.

"The One Where Joey Comes Back From LA,"
S10E12, *F·R·I·E·N·D·S*, by Ernesto DeRosa (excerpt)

INT. CENTRAL PERK COFFEESHOP – DAY
GUNTHER HANDS ROSS A CUP OF COFFEE OVER
THE COUNTER WHICH HE BRINGS TO THE
COUCH WHERE PHOEBE AND CHANDLER ARE
SITTING. ROSS IS WEARING LARGE PINK SWIM
GOGGLES ON HIS FOREHEAD.

CHANDLER
Have a seat, Aquaman.

ROSS
What?

PHOEBE
I don't think he realizes.

ROSS
Realizes what?

CHANDLER
Honestly, don't worry about it. Stay focused on the task
at hand. (BEAT) Looking for sunken treasure.

ROSS
(TOUCHES HIS FOREHEAD AND TAKES OFF THE
GOGGLES)

Oh man, I forgot to take them off after the gym again. I wore these on the subway!

JOEY WALKS IN THE DOOR, HIS CLOTHES DIRTY AND HAIR A MESS. HE SMILES AT HIS FRIENDS, REVEALING A MISSING TOOTH.

JOEY
I'm back guys! You have no idea what I've just been through.

PHOEBE
You seem to be forgetting a lot of things lately, Ross.

JOEY
(SITS DOWN IN EMPTY CHAIR BY COUCH)
Guys, I'm back!

ROSS
You're telling me. Last week, I forgot to bring my notes to class and had to deliver a three-hour lecture on an Archie comic I happened to have in my briefcase.

JOEY
Hello? Can anyone hear me? Anyway, listen to this. So things didn't go quite as planned in Los Angeles...

FADE TO:
INT. AIRPLANE
JOEY LOOKS OUT PLANE WINDOW.

JOEY (V.O.)

As you guys know, I flew down to LA to confront Todd Cowell. Remember, he's the big producer of *Days of Our Lives*? I was so mad the whole flight, like how can he cancel this classic show? Especially right after I come back as my old character, Dr. Drake Ramoray.

CUT TO:
EXT. LAX AIRPORT
JOEY'S PLANE LANDS.

JOEY (V.O.)

I had all this stuff ready that I was gonna say, about how I really needed the part and how it's this beloved soap opera. I just wanted to talk to the guy, man to man, and try and make him see why cancelling *Days of Our Lives* would be a bad idea.

CUT TO:
EXT. SUNSET STRIP – DAY
JOEY RIDES IN A TAXI, LOOKING OUT THE WINDOW AS HE CRUISES THE STRIP.

JOEY (V.O.)

Maybe I was losing my mind to think I could save the show. My back was still messed up from tripping over Emma's stroller and I was taking a lot of painkillers. I'm not sure what I was thinking. But anyway, as it turns out, the address my agent Estelle gave me was for the wrong Todd Cowell!

CUT TO:
EXT. TODD'S HOUSE – DAY
THE TAXI PULLS AWAY, LEAVING JOEY IN FRONT
OF A SMALL BUNGALOW. A HOMELESS MAN
DRAGS A GARBAGE BAG DOWN THE SIDEWALK
AND A SIREN RINGS IN THE DISTANCE.

JOEY (V.O.)
It didn't seem like the kind of place a big *Days of Our Lives* producer would choose to live in. Just a small house in a nothing neighborhood. No fancy cars in the driveway, no fountains or statues.

CUT TO:
EXT. TODD'S HOUSE – NIGHT
JOEY PEERS THROUGH A WINDOW.

JOEY (V.O.)
I did some surveillance and saw that it wasn't the right guy. It was some old man. I had driven all that way, though, so I went and booked a motel room.

CUT TO:
INT. MOTEL ROOM – DAY
JOEY LIES IN BED, WATCHING *DAYS OF OUR LIVES* ON TV.

JOEY (V.O.)
I still had some money left over from Dr. Drake Ramoray's first paycheque. I figured I could stay in Los

Angeles for a few more nights and try and get Estelle to figure out the real Todd Cowell's address. (BEAT) Estelle wasn't answering her phone. I called and I waited but nothing. And with these long-distance calls and the motel and the flight, plus all the money I gave Estelle earlier to track down Todd? (BEAT) I was broke.

CUT TO:
EXT. MOTEL PARKING LOT – DAY
JOEY WALKS OUT OF THE MOTEL AND THROUGH THE PARKING LOT, TOWARDS THE BUSY STREETS OF LA.

JOEY (V.O.)
I had nothing. No money, no food, no place to stay. I was out on the street. And then I remembered Todd Cowell. Not the producer guy, the old man.

CUT TO:
EXT. TODD'S HOUSE – NIGHT
JOEY WALKS UP THE DRIVEWAY TO THE WINDOW HE HAD PEERED THROUGH EARLIER, POPS OUT THE SCREEN AND CLIMBS INTO TODD'S HOUSE.

JOEY (V.O.)
I figured an old man would go to bed early and would probably have hearing problems, so what would be the big deal if I went and stayed at his place?

CUT TO:

INT. TODD'S KITCHEN – NIGHT

JOEY DRINKS MILK STRAIGHT FROM THE CARTON THEN PUTS THE CARTON IN THE FRIDGE. HE STRETCHES, YAWNS, CLIMBS INTO A CUPBOARD BENEATH THE SINK AND SHUTS THE DOOR.

JOEY (V.O.)

Just somewhere safe where I could crash until I figured out what to do—until I heard back from Estelle. I had to sleep in a cupboard in case the old man came out in the middle of the night and caught me. Obviously, this wasn't good for my sore back. On top of that I ran out of my painkillers.

JOEY CRAWLS OUT OF THE CUPBOARD AND WINCES, HOLDING HIS BACK.

JOEY (V.O.) (CONT'D)

I was sleeping in a cramped little kitchen cupboard every night and going through withdrawal from my back medicine at the same time. It was rough. One night I even took a bite out of a battery I found on Todd's counter.

JOEY PICKS A BATTERY OFF THE COUNTER, TAKES A BITE AND WINCES.

JOEY (V.O.)

I thought it was a baby carrot! I lost a tooth.

CUT TO:
EXT. SUNSET STRIP – DAY
JOEY WALKS THE STRIP HOLDING A WAD
OF BLOODY KLEENEX TO HIS MOUTH AND
LIMPING SLIGHTLY.

JOEY (V.O.)
So during the day I'd wander the streets aimlessly. I was
broken. I began to write an original *Days of Our Lives*
script so I could show Todd Cowell that there was still life
to the show. Of course, this was just further delusion. The
show would be cancelled. I had failed. (BEAT) And I realized something then, walking those streets. It didn't matter
if the show came to an end. That's not what's important.

FADE TO:
INT. CENTRAL PERK COFFEESHOP – DAY

JOEY
You guys are important. You three, plus Rachel and
Monica. My best friends. You're all that matters to me,
not some acting role. Now you want to know how I got
back home?

PHOEBE
Alright, I should get going. I've got a date with that
magician tonight!

CHANDLER
Make sure he doesn't try to saw you in half.

ROSS
I should get going too.

CHANDLER
Meeting Jughead for burgers, Ross?

ROSS
Very funny.

JOEY
Guys?

PHOEBE, CHANDLER AND ROSS EXIT.

JOEY
What's going on? Where are you going? Can anyone hear me? Guys?

FADE TO BLACK

◆

Five weeks after Ted Cohen put him in a coma, DeRosa woke up. A nurse called and Ted immediately drove to Cedars–Sinai.

Ted was relieved. This was what he had been waiting for. But another part of him, the part that had grown fond of the afternoons talking to the lifeless Texan in room B300, was disappointed it was over. As well, he lost his urge to yell, to lecture after reading the script he'd found in DeRosa's jacket. There was something so vulnerable about the Joey character that Ted's anger was replaced with feelings of sympathy. He worried for the schmuck.

Ted had his questions, though. Even more questions after having read the script. He wanted to know if DeRosa was really an actor who'd mistaken Ted for a TV producer and what he did back in Texas, if he was in fact from Texas; where his family was, what he'd do next and if he wanted his tooth back. All the blind spots that had been giving him a headache since the incident would soon be illuminated.

When Ted arrived at the hospital, Dr. Ramirez said DeRosa was doing well, given the circumstances. There was some minor brain damage but overall it looked like he would be fine. DeRosa had been awake for only a few minutes that morning but each day those few minutes would gradually stretch into hours, until eventually he'd be back to normal. The doctor said they needed to watch him closely and run some tests but that Ted was permitted to a moment with the patient. Ted went into the room and sat with DeRosa. DeRosa was asleep, but Ted spoke to him anyway. He described his car.

Every day that week, Ted drove to Cedars–Sinai. He'd tell the man in the bed what he had for breakfast that day, whether it was cereal or toast with jam, what he'd dreamt the night before and what the weather was doing. Sometimes DeRosa would open his eyes but he wouldn't speak. The same thing had happened with Ted's wife Annie before she'd died; one day she just stopped responding to Ted's questions but he knew she was listening because her eyes were open. DeRosa wasn't dying, however. It was Annie's situation in reverse—DeRosa was coming back. And the following week, on a Thursday morning, he spoke. Ted was sitting in a chair telling DeRosa how the hospital had finally reached his family—his ex-wife and son had been away in Europe—and that they were on their way to Los Angeles when DeRosa finally spoke.

"Your son's coming here, DeRosa," Ted said. "You'll probably see him tomorrow."

DeRosa coughed.

"DeRosa?"

"You're Ted Cohen," DeRosa said.

"Yes. I'm Ted Cohen and you're DeRosa."

"What day?"

"It's October. October the eighth."

"No. Day of the week."

"Oh. It's Thursday."

"Thursday."

"Thursday."

DeRosa went quiet again, his cardiac monitor filling the lull.

"Is there TV?" DeRosa said suddenly.

"In here? In your room? Yes," Ted said.

"Is there cable?"

"I think so. I'd have to check, but last time..."

"Can you come back?"

"What?"

"Can you come back tonight? For eight?"

Ted checked with the nurse when he left. She said the arrangement would be okay so he returned to Cedars–Sinai that night. As instructed, he rolled the TV up beside the bed and turned it to NBC for eight o'clock. The show had all the same characters as the postcard script. It was pretty good, Ted thought. This DeRosa guy wasn't so bad. Ted liked hanging around his bed; it was probably the first time he'd enjoyed someone else's company since Annie. DeRosa wasn't speaking, but he was awake. His eyes were wide for the duration of the show.

When the credits rolled at the end of the episode, Ted looked over towards the bed and saw that DeRosa was crying.

"Hey, easy there," Ted said. "It's okay, DeRosa. Where's the clicker? Something else will come on. We'll watch something else now."

He found the clicker on the floor and quickly turned the channel to a cooking show. A fat man dicing onions. DeRosa eventually stopped crying and went back to sleep. Ted felt himself drifting off too. He put his feet up along the side of the bed and slouched back. Why not, he thought. A nurse would wake him up.

"Good night, DeRosa," he said. "Thanks for having me over."

DeRosa's monitor beeped.

SPIRIT PALS

So things with Dad are kind of out of control. When's the last time you talked to Mom? You should really call her, Jane.

You have no idea. You remember how that house on our old street was burglarized earlier this year and how Dad started freaking out? He's worse. Mom doesn't know what to do. You really should give her a call, Jane.

Well I guess he bought all these cameras and floodlights and put heavy duty locks on the doors. Which is whatever. A little paranoid but makes some sense. But for some reason he bought cameras and everything for Mom and Tyler too. For Tyler's place which is kind of weird. Like, the guy's sleeping with his wife and now Dad's supplying their security equipment? Just bizarre. Hold on a sec…

Sorry, cat wanted in. So, yeah…

What? I've had him for three years, Jane! You must have met him before. George. When you were here in the spring. How do you not know I have a cat?

Anyway, so Dad became obsessed with his home security system with the cameras and everything. And it was all somewhat normal but then he got this BEWARE OF DOG sign.

No, he didn't get a dog—it was like a ruse.

A *ruse*. So people breaking in would think there was a dog.

Exactly. And that's fine too but then I guess he cut out a piece of the sign in the shape of bite marks. It was supposed to look like this big dog had bitten off the corner of the sign.

I don't know. I think it was meant to be the sort of thing where a potential burglar sees the sign and the bite marks and on some subconscious level thinks there is this wild dog living there with giant teeth that will attack anything. Like a dog that eats its own cautionary sign.

Right. And from there, things started getting really weird. I can't believe you don't know any of this. He's completely lost it. I mean, this is coming from Mom but still—you can kind of picture him doing this stuff now. So listen. After Dad cut the bite marks out of the sign, he decided to take it even further. Tried to pump up the illusion of this large, psychopathic dog living in his yard. Apparently he got hold of an official carrier's bag from Canada Post and attached it to the front lawn along with all these envelopes and junk mail.

Not kidding, yes. *Attached*. He put, I guess, little nails through each envelope and flyer and of course the mail bag so everything would stick to the lawn and not blow away. According to Mom it's all still in the yard. The desired effect of this little display being, I don't know, that someone about to break in will see the dog sign and all the mail stuff strewn about and then think that this vicious dog attacked or maybe even killed the mailman. I'm trying to get Mom to take pictures and send them to me but she keeps forgetting. Oh yeah, have you been getting these emails from Tyler?

I knew it. What do yours say?

Yeah, mine were pretty much the same. Like, super religious and creepy. And how our "new family direction" is God's will and that he's praying for me and my "spirit voyage" every day. You can see this stuff starting to influence Mom too. Last week she said that you and I need to look out for each other because siblings are "spirit pals" riding the same "voyage bus" or something. You should definitely call her after we're done. Have you been to Tyler's church?

No, it's a virtual church. You go to this website and enter all your personal information. It's like fifty bucks a month. And then you build a character—Mom's is a Pegasus, I think—and then all the parishioners log on with their characters every Sunday morning for Tyler's sermon. Which he, like, types into a chat bar.

I know. Definitely go check it out after we're done talking; I'll send you the link. So creepy. But back to Dad—so after the mailman thing he decided to turn the old shed into this huge doghouse. He took out the sliding doors and put a big piece of wood in their place with a doghouse-style door hole, rounded at the top. Then he drove a stake into the ground and tied a heavy chain to it which leads inside the shed. As if anyone would believe there's an enormous dog living in there.

Oh! And you remember his old footbath? For his corns? So he painted that red and put it outside the "doghouse." Wrote REX on the side of the footbath, like it's supposed to be this outlandish food bowl. Seriously, seriously. And listen, if that wasn't crazy enough, he found a pair of antlers somewhere—like the antlers from a stuffed deer, I guess—and placed them in the footbath so they'd stick out over the edge. The implication being, what? That this giant dog ate an entire deer? I need to get those pictures from Mom.

I will. God, Christmas is going to be so weird. You're coming down right? I think Ryan wants to drive so we can probably pick you up in Kingston on the way. Mom wants us to stay at Tyler's but I think Dad is kind of expecting us to go home.

So embarrassing, I know.

But wait, there's more. So Dad started this Neighbourhood Watch group which *sounds* great except everyone on his street thinks he's nuts now because of the dog stuff and so it's just him and his friend Phil. He's the one I used to babysit for with the twins? His wife left him too, and Mom says he's selling these crystals online now.

I don't know, they're supposed to have healing properties. But anyway, it's just Dad and Phil who have this Neighbourhood Watch thing and apparently they have drills where, like, Dad will break into Phil's house and Phil will break into Dad's house to test their security systems. Except Dad gave Phil a concussion one night when Phil was climbing through the kitchen window so I think they stopped doing that. What's that noise? Are you at a bar?

Right, the TV...

No, I'm just giving you a hard time. I remember *my* second year of university. But I hope you're not drinking too much, Jane. Mom's worried, just so you know. I guess she saw this thing on the news about binge drinking in dorm rooms and is convinced it was a sign from God that you're in trouble. Or maybe she said your "voyage" is in trouble.

No, I said you were fine, don't worry. You're fine, right?

Oh! You won't believe this: Dad's been wearing a ski mask to bed.

Ski mask, yes. And he has this burlap sack he keeps on his nightstand, so that if someone breaks in he'll get up and come out of the bedroom with the sack and his mask pulled down and then the intruder will think Dad's robbing the house too—and then I don't know. He'll say something like, "I was here first," so the other robber will leave. Or maybe Dad thinks he and the robber will work it out so that they split the things they end up stealing and then Dad will only lose half of what he would have lost if he hadn't tricked the other guy. So he can cut his losses.

Seriously.

No, I haven't talked to Dad in forever but Mom talks to him. She bought him a character in Tyler's church—says what he really needs is *spiritual* security—but he won't use the internet because he's afraid of hackers.

Well, call him if you want to but I don't think it's

so bad if you don't. I don't call him because he doesn't call me and plus last time I did he spent the whole conversation asking about our security system. I was like, "Dad, people don't even lock their front doors in my neighbourhood," which really got him going. Right after that he mailed me a jacket. Did you get one, too?

Well, it was just a normal spring jacket but he sewed the letters DEA onto it. There was a note in the package instructing me to hang it over the back of a chair in my kitchen, so that if anyone broke in they'd see it and think they were in this drug enforcement guy's house and run off shitting their pants. Do we even have a DEA in Canada? Ryan wore the jacket for Halloween last week with sunglasses and a phone cord going from his collar to his ear. I was Stevie Nicks. What did you end up doing?

That sounds like fun, Janie. But you're not drinking too much, are you? Because I remember when I was...

I know, I know. Mom and I are just worried. But obviously she's the more paranoid one and I'm only making sure that you're okay.

I know, I know. But anyway, we'll have to talk about Christmas. It's so weird how only a few years ago we were this somewhat normal family, you know? And now Mom is living with another man and is part of this online cult and Dad's wearing a balaclava to bed. I remember when we were kids and I thought Mom and Dad were these godlike people. Now it's like I'm the parent.

Like *we're* the parents, I mean.

Yeah, so I was thinking maybe we could stay in a hotel for Christmas. I don't really want to stay at Tyler's because obviously that would be weird—did you know he drives around on a *moped*? And who knows what Dad will try and pull if we go home. Or, like, if his friend Phil will try and break in while we're sleeping. We'll just get a hotel and tell them it's because we didn't want to pick favourites or something, I don't know. What's all that shouting in the background? Jane, are you at a bar?

I believe you, it just sounds like you're at a bar is all. Maybe turn the TV down. Anyway, I should go. Ryan's home. We'll talk about the hotel thing later and make sure you call Mom.

No, I won't tell her. But does that mean you *are* at a bar? You can tell me, I don't care.

Fine, sorry.

Okay, I gotta go.

Okay.

Call Mom.

Okay, bye.

THE FIDDLER MURDERS

got the idea from this know-it-all from work named Cathy. I sit beside her at the call centre because she's my age and the least sketchy person there. She wears nice skirts and blouses to work and gets her hair done once a month. You make do with what you're given. One weekend, Cathy went on a trip to Niagara-on-the-Lake with her husband and told me everything about it when she returned. They'd gone on a wine tour with bicycles and ate all this great food. They saw a musical, *Fiddler on the Roof,* and even dressed up for it. She talked about her trip all day. She rarely shuts her mouth.

When I left work at five, Cathy's story slipped my mind and I put my attention toward other things. There was dinner to prepare, for example. When I went to bed that night, though, I thought about Niagara-on-the-Lake. It sounded so nice. I liked how the town was on-the-lake. I wanted to ride bicycles and visit vineyards and put the bottles right in the bike basket. I wanted to see *Fiddler on the Roof*—I wanted to dress up. For the next few days it was all I thought about.

I brought the idea up at dinner one night. Orin, my husband, was complaining about his allergies and I interrupted him.

"Niagara," I said.

"Niagara," Orin said. "Is that like Claritin?"

"No, the town. Niagara-on-the-Lake. I think we should go there."

"We don't have any money. And don't interrupt me, it's rude. I'm saying we need to take all the plants out of the house. Just please put them on the back deck or I'll throw them in the garbage. It's got to be your damn plants that are driving me nuts and I need my eight hours, Laura."

"It's not the plants. But anyway, Cathy…"

"How do you know it's not the plants? Are you my doctor? No, you're not."

"I want to go to Niagara-on-the-Lake."

"Forget it."

I couldn't forget it, though. I imagined Cathy enjoying her vacation and I wanted to enjoy one too. Of course, I couldn't tell Cathy I was going on the same trip because she'd say I was stealing her idea. She's that kind of person. If I missed work to go, I'd have to tell her I was sick and watching movies at home with Orin. She probably wouldn't listen to me anyway.

Eventually, Orin said we could go. I had to ask him while he was drunk to get the answer I wanted. He came home from a meeting one night all puffy and loud and kept trying to pull me into the bedroom. I opened a bottle of wine, sat him down at the kitchen table and started selling him the trip.

"You can ride horses there," I said.

"I've always wanted to ride a horse," he said.

"When I was a kid I went to summer camp and they had horses but I never got to ride one."

"Well here's your chance."

"One of the horses at the camp came down with a neurological disease and acted crazy. They wouldn't let us kids ride any of the horses in case the others had the disease too. We went over to the stables to see them one day and this one horse was scraping his face against a tree. There was blood all over his face. I was ten years old."

"And it won't be that much money. We can drive there and stay some place cheap. Cathy's hotel was right on the water and they got a really good deal, she said." I made that part up, but it was probably true. There was always some kind of deal on the internet, I figured.

"On the last day of camp the horse tried to jump the fence and his legs got all tangled up in the wires. They had to shoot it. We all heard the shot while we were in the mess hall eating spaghetti."

"So it's settled."

We left the following weekend. It should have been a four-hour drive from Windsor but Orin had to stop every twenty minutes, or so it seemed. He didn't have a bowel movement that day, which was an unusual thing. Orin had a bowel movement every morning at nine a.m. for the past thirty years, he claimed. And now, nothing.

"I will *not* be constipated on this trip, Laura," he said.

We stopped near Chatham, London, Woodstock, Brantford, Hamilton and St. Catharines. Orin would go into the washroom and I'd sit in the car and wait for ten or fifteen minutes. It became a predictable pattern that when Orin came out of a washroom and walked towards the car, he'd put up his hands and shake his head so I'd know he'd failed in there.

"Maybe I need to eat some fruit," he'd say once he was back in the car. Or, "What about figs?" Or, "Maybe I need to lie down in the back seat and massage my stomach for a while."

"What about we just drive to Niagara already?" I said, at one of the stops.

"What about I take us back home?"

I kept my mouth shut.

We were mostly silent for the rest of the drive. I flipped on the radio at one point and Orin flipped it right back off. I didn't press him. I wanted to get to Niagara-on-the-Lake before it got dark.

I looked out my window and watched the landscape barely change. It was all fields and strip malls. I saw a billboard advertising "knuckle spray," whatever that was. I probably read it wrong.

When we approached the Niagara region, however, there were ridges and hills and rivers. It was beautiful. We drove over a bridge that felt like it was the Golden Gate it was so big. I'd never been on the

Golden Gate and knew it was probably ten or twenty times the size as whatever bridge we were on, but still. I was excited. I did a little dance in my seat.

"For Christ's sake, Laura," Orin said. "I'm driving. You're gonna break the seat."

It was dark by the time we reached Niagara-on-the-Lake. Our hotel was decent, but it smelled slightly of rotten bananas. The kid behind the desk was asleep in his chair—we had to wake him up to get our room key. The first thing Orin wanted to do when we got to our room was use the bathroom. Despite the frequent rest stops, my husband hadn't had his bowel movement yet.

There was a Jacuzzi tub in our room with a piece of paper taped to it: DO NOT USE. The bathroom had sliding windows above the Jacuzzi which opened into our room. Like, you could sit in the tub with the windows open and see the bed or watch TV while you bathed—if the tub actually worked, you could. These sliding windows wouldn't close properly, though, and Orin said he couldn't shit with me in the room so I had to wait in the hall.

I sat out there for ten minutes or so wondering if Cathy had had these tub windows which wouldn't quite close. Or if she had to wait in a hallway for her husband to use the toilet. Orin came out of the room to get me with his hands up, shaking his head.

"I can't go if you're just out here waiting for me," he said. "You need to be doing something. Not just waiting around."

"What should I do?" I said.

"For Christ's sake, I don't know. But don't stand out here waiting around. It makes me nervous. I will *not* be constipated the whole trip."

I went down to the lobby and looked at the pamphlets. Most of them were for attractions in Niagara Falls, which Cathy said were overpriced. I found a pamphlet for a bicycle tour. There were pictures of couples cycling down country roads with wine bottles in their bike baskets. A woman in one of the photos looked a little like Cathy—they both had blonde pixie cuts and long, elegant faces—and I could picture the guy in the photo being Cathy's husband, whom I'd never met. I fantasized about going on the bicycle tour the next day and how maybe someone would take our picture and put it in a pamphlet. I'd get Orin to wear the nice shirt he'd brought for *Fiddler* just in case. I'd wear my blue dress. I'd keep my chin up if there was a photographer shooting us so you couldn't see my neck fat in the photo.

I picked out a few other pamphlets and read through them: there was a day spa, a tea room, a paranormal museum, a newspaper museum, the horse stables and the theatre house where Cathy and her husband had gone. I put the pamphlets in order from must-see to maybe-if-there's-time. I drummed my fingers on the pamphlet stand. Half an hour passed without Orin. I went back upstairs to find he had fallen asleep on the bed.

Cathy texted me while I was lying in the dark playing Tetris on my phone.

Hope yr feeling ok Laura

I replied that I was still pretty sick but Orin and I were at home watching a movie.

What movie? she wrote back.

I thought for a minute.

Miss congeniality

Oooo what channel? Im so bored

Actually its a dvd

Can I borrow when yr back at work?

Sure

So now I'd have to go and buy it.

I went back to Tetris and played until my eyes ached. I closed them and waited for sleep.

"You need to get up, Laura," a voice said. I opened my eyes and there was Orin hovering over me. A pale light shone through the curtains.

"What's..."

"You need to get up. I think I can go now but I can't go with you in the room. Quick, before it goes away."

"You didn't go last night?"

"No. Hurry up, before it goes away. And don't just stand in the hallway. Go outside or something."

I stood up, pulled on a sweater and went down to the lobby.

A woman was behind the reception desk this time and the banana smell was gone. She was talking to an old man with keys on his belt and they both wore serious expressions. They were leaning over a newspaper that was spread out on the desk. I went over to the pamphlet stand and listened in.

"So sad," the woman said. "Did you know them?"

"No. I saw the guy around though. Last week at the bank. Funny, Mary and I were supposed to go see it tomorrow. It would've been the last show of the run, but I guess they're shutting down. Obviously."

"I know. So sad."

I could have just asked them what had happened but I felt too embarrassed to talk to anyone the way I was dressed. I looked around the lobby for another newspaper but couldn't find one. Then I noticed the *Niagara Advance* box out on the street.

I stepped outside and read the headline through the plastic window on the door: FIDDLER ON THE ROOF DIRECTOR AND STAR FOUND DEAD IN CAR. I didn't have my wallet with me to buy a copy so I just stood there and read what I could through the window. Apparently, the woman directing the musical that Orin and I were planning to see that night, as well as the guy who played the role of Tevye, were shot in the actor's car outside of the theatre after last night's performance. There were no suspects so far. That's all I could read.

The thing I'd been looking forward to the most, the musical, had been pulled from the menu. I cursed my luck. Of course, I felt terrible for the poor people who had been murdered but I just wanted to see a nice performance.

Two cop cars drove by. I went back inside the hotel.

Upstairs, Orin was lying on the bed and rubbing his stomach.

"Did you go yet?" I said.

"What do you think?"

"Hey, you'll never guess what happened. Last..."

"Did I take a shit?"

"What?"

"Did I take a shit? Is that what you're about to tell me? Unless you're going to tell me I took a shit, I don't care."

"That doesn't make sense, Orin."

We dressed and left to find breakfast.

We found a place nearby but Orin wouldn't touch his eggs. He said they looked too yellow. Then he asked our server if she could turn the music down—admittedly, it was a little much—and she did but her mood changed after that. She didn't look at us when she came by our table to refill the water glasses. Orin refused to leave her a tip when we left but I snuck a five under my plate while he wasn't looking.

We went back to the hotel to ask about the wine tour. We'd missed it. The lady at the desk said the guy comes by with the bus to pick people up at seven every morning—it was already eleven. She said we could go tomorrow, but we'd have to be ready by seven this time. Seven *sharp*, she said.

"I didn't like her tone," said Orin when we returned to our room. "She acted like we were her kids or something. How the hell are we supposed to know when the damn bus comes? And why is there a bus? I thought this was a bicycle thing."

"He has to drive us out to the vineyards first. He has the bikes and everything. Stop being so negative. She didn't mean anything."

"Like hell she didn't."

"Orin, you're being ridiculous." I said but didn't really think he was. I wasn't fond of the desk lady myself. We weren't her damn kids.

Later that day, Orin still hadn't had his bowel movement but I convinced him to go to the horse stables in the afternoon. We drove to a ranch just outside of town where there was an amazing trot path that went by a little waterfall. We paid and got all set up but then Orin wouldn't get on his horse.

"I don't like the look of mine," he said.

"Well then let's trade."

"No, you go ahead. I don't really like the look of either of them."

I didn't want to ride alone so we just went back to the hotel. Orin made me wait in the hall for a while and then we took a nap.

We had the TV on while we were dressing for dinner

and I noticed there was an update on the "Fiddler Murders," which was what they were calling them. It was a national news story now. There were still no suspects but there had been another unsolved car shooting in Niagara Falls a month earlier. A woman waiting for her son to get off work was gunned down by the side of the road—probably by the same killer.

The TV reporter was standing outside the theatre and cops and news trucks were all around. They had yellow police tape up and people were crowding behind it, watching the scene. The caption at the bottom of the screen read: "*Fiddler on the Roof* murderer on the loose in Niagara-on-the-Lake."

"That's kinda funny," Orin said.

"How is that funny?" I said. "Two people died last night."

"The caption. You can't tell me that's not funny. I think it's *meant* to be a little funny."

"It's not funny." I was lying... it was a little funny. But it was funny to appreciate on the inside and keep to yourself because two people had been killed and it wasn't right to laugh at that kind of thing.

The streets were busy and we had to wait twenty-five minutes for a table at the restaurant I'd picked. We waited at the bar and everyone was talking about the *Fiddler* murders. One guy said he'd sold the woman, the director, a pack of cigarettes the day she died. Another said he figured the killer was someone local who auditioned for a role in the musical but didn't make the cut—or maybe was an understudy. And then a woman said it was great they had all this publicity for the musical now but that it was useless because they'd shut down the production. Orin and I sat and listened.

The server came to escort us to our table but by the time I arrived I couldn't find Orin. He'd just slipped off. I sat down anyway and told the server my husband would be back, and he did come back ten minutes later. He walked towards the table with his arms up, but with a big grin.

"I made!" he said.

"Oh, I'm so glad, dear."

"Things will be different now. We can really start our vacation. I bet I could hop on a horse right now. Are they still open?"

"Oh, I'm so happy."

It was the best dinner. I ordered pasta and Orin had roast duck and scalloped potatoes. We shared a bottle of Pinot Noir from one of the local vineyards— one we'd probably visit the next day on the tour. Our server was charming and the music was at the perfect volume. I couldn't stop smiling.

We talked about the wine tour and Orin suggested we stay an extra day so we could visit the stables again.

"I'm getting on that horse, Laura," Orin said. "You can count on that."

"We'll ride past the waterfall."

"You bet your little ass we will."

When we got back to the hotel I thought we were going

to have sex. We were tipsy from the wine and Orin groped me a little in the elevator. A married couple doesn't need to have sex all the time but when you're staying in a hotel I think it's important to have sex at least once. Especially if you've had a nice time at dinner. But when I went into the washroom to change out of my blue dress, Orin fell asleep. I sat on the bed beside him and played Tetris on my phone.

We woke up at eight—we'd missed the pickup for the bicycle tour. It was raining anyway.

"Maybe we should just drive home," Orin said.

"What about the horses?"

"It's raining."

"I thought we were going to stay another day?"

"It's *raining*, Laura."

We left after Orin's nine a.m. bowel movement.

The rain stopped around Hamilton and it was clear skies all the way until Windsor. We didn't say much to each other. Orin let me play the radio for a bit. There was more news about the *Fiddler* murders: Still no suspects, but apparently the police found an unlicensed gun and half an ounce of crystal meth in the director's car. It was too early to speculate, the newswoman said, but she speculated anyway. She said it was possible the two victims were involved with some sort of crime ring. It was all very sensational but Orin made me shut the radio off because he had a headache.

I wondered what Cathy would say when I returned

to work the next day. She'd probably go on about how she'd just been there, in Niagara-on-the-Lake, and how she'd seen the musical with the two murder victims. She'd act like the office expert on the whole matter. If anyone brought it up, Cathy would swoop in and take over the conversation: *Well, when I saw the production*, I could imagine her saying, *I noticed something a little off about the guy playing Tevye.* I bet you did, Cathy.

The funny thing was that I was actually there for the whole murder. I could have sat next to the killer in a restaurant, or maybe they were staying in our hotel. You never know. But I couldn't say anything because Cathy thought I was sick at home. My Niagara-on-the-Lake story was better and more relevant than hers even though Orin and I didn't really do much. We didn't do anything aside from our dinner. But we were there. And it was a magical dinner.

"Remember dinner last night?" I said. We were outside of Woodstock.

"It was good."

"I really had a great time with you, Orin."

"The food was excellent."

We stopped for lunch in London and Orin let me run into Wal-Mart afterwards. I went to the DVD section to look for *Miss Congeniality* so I could lend it to Cathy but they didn't have it. I found the movie version of *Fiddler on the Roof* in a bargain bin, which I bought. I missed out on the live show but I could have my own private experience when we got home to supplement the trip.

I couldn't wait to get back home and watch the film. I scanned the DVD case for the rest of the drive to Windsor imagining what the film would be like. It's exciting to watch something that's relevant to your own experiences. The whole thing would be coloured by the murders.

We stopped for the last time before arriving home near Chatham. Orin filled up the car and I bought an ice cream sandwich. I ate half and passed the rest to Orin.

The next day at work I didn't say a word to Cathy about any of it. I let her yammer on about a painting class she'd signed up for. I smiled and nodded along. She had no idea where I'd been.

"The instructor's actually from Paris?" I said.

"He really is!" Cathy said.

But I wasn't listening to Cathy's story. I was thinking about Orin. I pictured him walking over to me in the restaurant, his hands up in the air, the enormous grin plastered across his face. I wanted to live inside that moment. Orin would never reach the table and we would never place our orders. But I wouldn't know that. I'd just sit and watch my smiling husband walk towards me forever.

POOL RULES

• No running on the pool deck.

• No splashing or horseplay.

• No flotation devices (except on Tube Night).

• Proper swim attire must be worn at all times. Bathing suits and swim caps with Sunny Planet Aquatic Centre insignia can be purchased at the front desk. Do not enter pool area unless you are wearing these items.

• Patrons must shower before entering the pool. To turn on shower, enter your name and social security number into the touch-screen below shower head.

• Always swim with a buddy. You will be randomly paired with a swim buddy upon exiting the locker rooms. This person will be your permanent swim buddy. Pool Leader will perform a brief ceremony before you and your buddy may enter pool. Do not think of this as a "wedding," though legally you will be married to each other.

• No cursing.

• No English. Patrons must speak Korean until Pool Leader finalizes the unique Sunny Planet Aquatic Centre language.

• Refer to your swim buddy and the other patrons by their Pool Names only. If you are male, your Pool Name will be Marco. Females are named Polo. Do not forget your Pool Name.

• Do not attempt to climb on the lifeguard towers. Sunny Planet lifeguards are armed and extremely overworked—the stress of the long hours may cause resentment toward pool patrons.

• Do not look lifeguards in the eye.

• Before using the diving boards, patrons must sign a release form stating that Sunny Planet is not responsible for any injuries and that patrons promise to cut off all ties with their families.

• Please be advised: Sunny Planet Aquatic Centre has a Locked-In Policy, which means you cannot leave the premises until you complete our intensive water-safety training program. Bunks are provided in the locker rooms until training is completed.

• No outside food or drink is allowed. Use the wall-mounted food pellet machines if you are hungry. These machines only accept Cleaning Tokens, which you can earn by cleaning the facilities.

• Do not drink from the water fountains. The water in these fountains contains a highly concentrated poison and will serve its purpose at a later date.

• Every hour there is a mandatory group chant held in the lobby. If this is your first visit to Sunny Planet, you are required to bring all your possessions and add them to our "First-Timers" pyre which will be set ablaze by Pool Leader.

• Do not look Pool Leader in the eye.

• Respect the pool. Greet the pool before entering the water and thank the pool before exiting. One hour per day should be spent bent over in supplication before the pool.

• Do not enter the pool if you have any open sores or communicable diseases. The infected are not welcome at Sunny Planet Aquatic Centre. If you see an infected person approach the pool, inform a lifeguard immediately and stand out of the way.

• Use the waterslide with caution. You may notice that the waterslide does not appear to lead into the pool but instead appears to travel through the adjacent wall.

Ignore this. This is an illusion due to the curves of the slide and light bouncing off the water.

• Do not knock on the windows at the bottom of the pool. Do not wave to the men in lab coats on the other side of the glass as they are very busy.

• If you notice the water in the pool change colour or turn opaque, do not panic. Do not exit the pool. Move to the centre of the pool where the men in lab coats can monitor your behaviour through the windows.

• Do NOT drink the pool water. If pool water is accidentally swallowed, signal to the men in lab coats and wait for assistance.

• Children under twelve must be supervised by an adult. They must also enroll in our special school. Transportation will be provided to our Sunny Planet Farm where the school grounds are located. Your child will be returned when he or she is of marriageable age.

• Lifeguards have full authority over pool patrons and may enforce rules not listed here, as needed. If approached by a lifeguard on the pool deck, lie down on your stomach and clasp your hands above your head.

• If you hear talk of a resistance movement, inform a lifeguard. There is no resistance movement and there is certainly no "chosen one." If you notice a voice coming from an air duct in the locker rooms claiming that you are the "chosen one," inform a lifeguard and proceed to the waterslide.

• Do not ask pool staff to open the retractable roof. The retractable roof will open in July of 2025 when the Mothership is expected to land.

• Should the Mothership arrive ahead of schedule, an ear-splitting alarm will sound. If you hear this alarm, exit the pool as it will be drained and converted into a landing pad. Put on your Sunny Planet flip-flops, queue up at one of the water fountains and await instructions from Pool Leader.

• Absolutely no Band-Aids in the pool. This is a shared space—be mindful.

BOWMAN

Charlie Eckles surveys his empire. The Good Morning breakfast diner. Sunday. A handful of customers but the church crowd would come rolling in shortly. This is *mine*, Eckles thinks. I built this. Six crummy booths. One long, crummy counter with eight crummy stools bolted to the floor. Two framed *Gone with the Wind* movie posters—he's never seen the film. Eight loaves of Dempster's Texas Toast. My legacy. Alexander the Great ruled over Macedonia, but Eckles the Underwhelming ruled the waffle iron.

"What am I looking at here?" Eckles steps back into the kitchen.

"Table four," Patty says. Patty's waited on Good Morning's customers since the place opened, five years ago. She saw the whole thing come together. Eckles owned it with his wife, Maureen. Instead of a honeymoon, Eckles always said, we decided to start a business. The two newlyweds got the restaurant up and running and then, one year in, Maureen took off with the neighbour. Last Eckles heard she was working a perfume counter in Vancouver.

"Table four, sure."

"You recognize that face?"

"Yeah, it's the new pope."

"It's Todd Bowman. Don't you read the paper?"

"You're pulling my leg." Eckles knows who Todd Bowman is. He read the paper. Todd Bowman, bank robber. Twenty-first-century outlaw. Wanted man. Hospitalized two security guards and a bank manager in Stratford just last week. Eckles saw the man's photograph that morning, skimmed the story. Cops were still searching, it said.

"Look again," Patty says.

Eckles pokes his head out into the front of the restaurant. Table four, there he is. Now that he knows what to look for, it's obvious. The busted nose. The long, greedy mouth. All those muscles crammed into the plastic booth. A caricature of a crook. The papers loved running Bowman photos on the front page.

"Jesus." Eckles ducks back into the kitchen, sits on a potato sack. "What do we do?"

"Can't call the cops," Brian the cook snorts.

"That's *exactly* what we should do," Patty says. "And let's keep our voices down."

"Just sayin'," Brian says. "If it really is Bowman and you bring the authorities down here, there'll be trouble. He'll tear this place apart."

Tear this place apart—the phrase begins to loop in Eckles' mind. Why didn't I think of that? he wonders. The restaurant had become a burden. A coffin. A symbol of his broken marriage. Of his defeat. While Maureen was off petting dolphins on the west coast, he was trapped in the diner sanitizing coffee mugs. Ordering napkins. Frying eggs. When he and Maureen decided to open the diner, they had a vision: a hub for the community, a spot where locals could meet up and chat with each other. The kind of place sitcom characters hung around—where narratives intersected and series regulars walked in the door to a studio applause. A place of comfort. That dream was long dead. Bowman ought to tear this dive apart, Eckles thinks. Perfect place for a shootout. And maybe I'll catch a stray bullet. Put me out of my misery.

"We have to call," Patty says. "It's our duty."

"Your duty," Eckles says, "is walking plates out to the customers. Anyway, are we sure it's him? Seems like a dumb move, coming in here."

"Absolutely it's him. The guy takes risks. That's his whole thing. Besides, it's just a phone call. The police can decide."

"Let's see what he tips first," Eckles says.

"This is serious."

"Alright, alright. I'll slip out back and call." Eckles peeks into the dining area—Bowman was still digging his way through the Farmboy Skillet—and pulls his phone from his apron. He steps out the back door into the parking lot and pauses. He calls back into the kitchen before closing the door behind him, "Is this a nine-one-one thing? I mean, would you call this an emergency?"

"Hmm." Patty shrugs. "I think so. Yes. Of course it is."

"Well, that's the number I know. Be right back."

The emergency dispatcher takes in Eckles' story, types his information into a computer and tosses him on hold. Spanish guitar music plays. Eckles didn't think they'd have hold music over at nine-one-one. Seems disrespectful. Disrespectful to whom, he isn't sure. Just disrespectful in general. At least play something with a steady beat, not this meandering dog shit, he thinks.

What am I doing here? Eckles thinks. Ratting on a customer. Sure, the man's dangerous. A scourge to society. But who am I to intervene? Guy comes in for a hot meal, I'm sending him up the river. I should be trying to hold on to the few customers I have, not getting them locked up. If I had any guts I'd be right there with Bowman. The man was free, truly free. No restrictions. Robbing banks. Driving around. Better than scraping grease spatter off the walls all day, that's certain. A woman comes on the line and asks the same questions as the dispatcher. Keys clack.

"Stay where you are, sir. Do not approach this man. A team is on its way now."

Eckles hangs up and moves back inside. *A team*, he thinks.

In the kitchen, Eckles sees Patty walking towards him from the dining room with a panicked expression on her face.

"He's gone," she says.

"Gone where?"

"Out the front door."

Eckles walks into the dining area. Table four, unoccupied. Deserted.

"Did he pay his bill?" Eckles asks.

"We can't let him get away," Patty says. "He could shoot someone. Kill them. And that'll be on us."

"The woman on the phone told me to stay where I was," Eckles protests. "She said not to approach Bowman. She said those words specifically."

"He's getting away. We need to see where he goes so we can tell the cops where to find him. You don't need to approach him. Just give me your keys if you're gonna be a baby about this."

There was no way he was letting Patty drive his car. The woman dropped dishes left and right, spilled coffee on laps. It was her nerves. One time Eckles watched Patty walk right into a wall. She was talking to a customer, head turned around. Thought she was headed for the kitchen and splat. If Eckles lent Patty his car, a crane would be pulling it from the lake within the hour. Besides, she had a point. Bowman might kill someone. They were already involved. He didn't want to look like a coward so he went.

Moments later, Eckles is behind the wheel of his Toyota Yaris cursing his staff. Cursing Patty specifically. Patty saw Bowman leave, saw him climb into a white Sierra pickup, saw him drive west on Main Street.

Eckles drives west on Main. He assumes Bowman is long gone. He hopes so too. The plan is to drive around the neighbourhood for twenty minutes, smoke a cigarette, listen to the radio and gas up the car. Then he'll head back and tend to the brunch crowd. A few hours of that headache, then home. Have a soak. Watch a documentary on the computer with a glass of wine. Something historical. Try and relax.

At the next stoplight, however, Eckles sees the white Sierra turning out of the Sunoco across the intersection. The timing's perfect. The light turns green and Eckles pulls up behind Bowman's truck as he leaves the station. Great, thinks Eckles. He holds back on the gas to put some distance between the two vehicles. Can't let this guy know he's being followed, which means, Eckles realizes, that he's now following Bowman. He's doing it. Actively pursuing a dangerous criminal. Tailing a perp. They're still driving west on Main. Eckles figures Bowman's headed for the 401. He could be going south to Windsor and then he'll attempt to cross the border. Or north, up to Toronto, to get lost in the big city. He likely has some hideout, some place inconspicuous out in the country. Could have a band of like-minded goons waiting for him at the hideout. Eckles pictures this—the dusty floors, the card tables, the cellar door leading to an elaborate torture chamber—and knows he's in over his head. I should have stayed at the diner, like the emergency dispatcher said. Should have stayed in bed. Should have stayed in the womb.

Eckles reaches for his phone. If he calls the diner he can tell Patty where he is. Get the police on the line.

They can use their roof lights, speed through traffic, catch up to him and take over the pursuit. Eckles can go back to work. The Good Morning hasn't seemed so inviting in years. Except he doesn't have his phone, Eckles realizes with disgust. It's in his apron. He hung the apron on the back of the door before leaving. Moron. He has no way of contacting anyone. A complete moron. He's alone in this.

Before they make it to the highway, Bowman turns right on Ajax, a country road surrounded by fields and forests. The two cars that had been driving between Bowman and Eckles continue straight—the buffer is gone. Eckles makes the right onto Ajax and now it's just the two of them. He slows down.

He'll continue the pursuit. Follow Bowman until he reaches his hideout or motel or wherever the hell he's headed for. Then drive to a gas station, coffee shop—anywhere with a phone. Then he'll call the police, relay the information and drive back to the diner. Receive his shiny medal. Easy.

Except, he realizes, Bowman just filled his tank. He could be going anywhere. Eckles is running low on fuel—real low. The needle's past E. If he turns around now he still might not make it back to the diner. And who knows what a lunatic like Bowman has in mind. In fact, maybe he's spotted Eckles already. Maybe Bowman *was* headed for the highway, but turned down Ajax to see if Eckles' Yaris was following him. Which it is. And, by making that turn he's just confirmed it. Bowman *knows*. And now they're alone.

The two vehicles continue down Ajax. They pass silos, thickets and a small lake. The sky is overcast, depressing. Leaves rot on the ground. There's no one else on the road. Eckles considers turning around. He can tell the police where Bowman's headed and say he lost him. Besides, why waste any more time on this? Eckles isn't going to stop a goddamn bank robber. If anyone's coming out of this situation on top, it's Bowman. The man who successfully robbed banks. The man who shot security guards and got away with it. Eckles has never got away with anything. No one put Eckles on the front page of the newspaper—he is a nothing. Maureen knew that. His own wife saw where he was headed in life, realized his limited potential and cut him loose. Smartest decision she ever made. Eckles knows his place.

Before he can make up his mind, Eckles sees the Sierra slow down. Good God, Eckles thinks. What's this maniac doing? The white truck pulls over to the side of the road. Eckles checks his rear-view—there's no one behind him. It's just Eckles and Bowman. There's nothing to do but drive on. He speeds up.

Eckles looks out the passenger window as he drives past Bowman. They meet eyes. Bowman's face is blank, serious, his hands resting on the steering wheel. "Oh shit," Eckles says. Once he's ahead of Bowman, Eckles checks the rear-view. The Sierra is moving again; it's following him.

Eckles squeezes the wheel as sweat drips through his knuckles. He belches—his breath smells like ketchup. He stares down the long, empty road. He's never driven out this way before and he's not sure where he's headed exactly. Toward Rodney? Bowman's Sierra is still behind him, otherwise there's no traffic. Eckles belches again. His guts feel like a closed fist. The engine sputters. The Yaris is handling all wrong, thirsty for fuel and slowly dying. Soon, the car will roll to a stop. And then he'll have to deal with Bowman.

The Sierra keeps its distance. Eckles thought Bowman would run him off the road, but he's holding back. A few minutes earlier, Eckles made a left turn on Telegraph Road and so did Bowman. There's nothing on Telegraph Road. Corn fields on one side, pine trees on the other and in Eckles' rear-view, the white Sierra— so far behind it's just a dot in the mirror. In a way, it's worse that Bowman's hanging back. Like he's playing a game. Moving all slow and confident. Like a villain. Like a goddamn cartoon.

The road stretches on as far as Eckles can see. No turns to make, just corn and pine trees. The engine's coughing and the car's lurching. He's not going to make it, Eckles realizes. This is it. He checks the rear-view one last time. White dot in the distance. He presses the gas to the floor, figuring one last burst of speed before the engine quits on him but nothing happens. It's dead. He's coasting. Might as well be fleeing the maniacal killer on a skateboard.

Eckles thinks suddenly of the corn. He can hide in the corn. No time to assess the idea or weigh its merits so Eckles simply acts. He cranks the steering wheel and veers off the road. The car crashes through the chicken wire fence. Eckles hits his head on the driver's window. There's a terrible scraping sound from underneath like the car's being ripped in half. Then the cracking of corn stalks, flattening before him in the windshield. He drifts into the cornfield, speed decreasing with each broken stalk, until the vehicle comes to a complete stop.

Eckles opens the door, shoving it hard against the corn so he can climb out and immediately starts running. Down the row, husks and leaves smack into his face. Broken stalks scrape his shins. He isn't sure if Bowman's in there with him but he dodges to the right, makes his way to another row and keeps running. He's out of breath. His briefs ride up into his butt crack. Chest pains. He keeps running.

Eventually, Eckles can't take anymore. He's been hoofing it through walls of heavy corn for ten, twenty minutes—he can't be sure. He stops. He's done. His heart pounds in his throat. He puts his hands on his knees, panting, and listens. A bird chirps somewhere. The corn stalks rustle in the wind, otherwise all is quiet. Eckles sits down in the mud and brings his hand to his head where it hurts. Where he hit it against the window coming in to the field. There's blood on his fingers. Is Bowman in here with me? he wonders. Waiting up ahead. I'll start walking and he'll jump out, slit my throat. But then again, why would he bother? Check the imbecile in the Yaris off your list, Bowman! He's probably miles from here by now. Laughing it up. Organizing his money piles. Another anecdote for his memoirs when he's finally locked up. Standing around in the yard with the other inmates. Tell that one about the idiot who drove into the corn-field again, Bowman.

Eckles stands. Wipes the dirt off his jeans. No sign of the bank robber, he walks through the corn. No sense in going back to the car—Bowman could be there waiting, sharpening his dagger on a rock—so he continues down the row, away from the road. Eckles thinks of Maureen. All that corn. She grew up on a farm, he thinks. Not too far from here. There was prob-ably corn throughout her childhood.

Eckles misses her. Actually misses her—not the usual self-pity. Misses seeing her and talking to her. If he makes it out of the field in one piece, he decides, he'll track down her number and call her. See how she's doing. It wasn't her fault, what happened. Sure, she left. But he practically shoved her out the door. Tried to control everything. The diner was all his idea. The wedding too. They had problems before she took off. Before they got hitched even. Communication prob-lems. Heated arguments. Mutual bitterness. Eckles tried to ignore their issues by throwing nuptials at them, covering everything up with work on the new restaurant. He had a thousand opportunities to mend things with Maureen but he chose to look the other way. He'd always felt that things fixed themselves, given enough time, but they don't.

A half hour passed by. Eckles' feet are sore and his breathing is laboured. He's thirsty and hungry. And then he steps out of the cornfield, onto the greenest grass he's ever seen.

Someone's yard. A small house a kilometre away. There's a truck in the driveway; it's blue. Eckles kicks clumps of mud from his sneakers and makes for the house. A small, old man in bifocals answers the door. He's wearing a baby blue cardigan and is smiling with his magnified eyes. Eckles smells something sweet and familiar coming from down the hall—waffles?

"Hello there," the old man says. "What are we selling today?"

"I'm sorry to bother you, sir," Eckles says. He looks down at his shoes. He feels like he's in trouble, like he's about to be disciplined. "I need to use your phone. I crashed my car into your corn."

"Oh Lord," the old man says, reaching for Eckles' arm. "Are you alright? Come in, come in. You can use the phone. Eileen! Eileen, there's a man here's had an accident. Eileen, get in here!"

Eckles calls nine-one-one again. He's transferred around from person to person and so ends up telling his story to three different people. When he hangs up, the old man wants to hear what happened too even though he'd sat there staring at him the whole time. So Eckles tells it again. Then Eileen comes into the living room with a basket of homemade apple fritters. The old man tells her the story now. Gets about half of it right. Calls Bowman "Darwin."

Eckles wonders what will happen to Bowman. Prison, most likely. Unless he's gunned down. It was inevitable. A lifestyle like that, your options begin to narrow. An hour ago, Eckles was thinking Bowman was truly free, unencumbered by laws, but the opposite was true. *Eckles* was free. If anything, there was *too many* directions he could take. All that freedom was overwhelming.

"Have another fritter," Eileen says. "Is someone coming to get you? Would you like some tea? I can put coffee on if you'd rather."

"I'm fine, thank you," Eckles says. "A detective is on his way here now. He'll take me back to town."

"I'll put on some coffee anyway. Maybe the detective wants coffee. I should make more fritters."

They're sitting on wicker chairs. A radio is playing in the kitchen, schmaltzy wartime music. The house smells like fried sugar and fresh laundry. Eckles can't stop eating the apple fritters. He's never been so hungry. He licks his fingers. The fritters are the most enjoyable meal he's had in his life. Eckles doesn't notice any pain, his headache's gone. The fear of Bowman is gone. All that is out the window. He's comfortable. The two old-timers have a calming presence. There's a painting of a German shepherd on the wall; that's calming too. The music. The fritters.

"Can I use your phone again?" Eckles asks.

"Eileen," the old man calls to the kitchen, "bring the phone in here."

Eckles calls the Good Morning and Patty answers

on the first ring. He tells her he's okay and gives her the basic story as quickly as he can because that's not the reason he's calling. Eckles wants to tell her the ideas he has for the diner. A new theme. New menu. He tells Patty to take notes. They'll rip out the booths and put in wicker tables and chairs. There will be new aprons for the staff. He'll paint the exterior blue. Eckles stares at the beautiful German shepherd on the wall and wonders what it'll take for the old man and Eileen to sell it to him.

ODE TO THE LIBRARY

You're wandering the downtown sidewalks looking for a place that's warm and quiet when you see a pretty girl crossing the street. *Where is she off to?* you wonder and so you follow. Maybe she knows of a nice spot where you can sit for a while and just as you think this she turns and walks into the library.

You've never been inside the library before and now you have to wonder why not because it's just the thing: literature, reference books, music, films, newspapers from around the world—thousands of ways to enrich and intoxicate the mind and all for the price of a promise that you'll bring it all back on time.

There's the pretty girl again, emerging from behind a shelf with a book in her hands. You follow her to the other side of the room where she places herself at a table and begins to read; you grab the nearest hardcover and sit where you can watch her. Her attention is rapt—what could she be reading? Who *is* she? She looks around and catches you staring so you quickly hide behind the pages of your own book, *Coping with Irritable Bowel Syndrome*. You blush and lay the book flat.

Half an hour passes. You steal glances at this captivating woman until she eventually gets up—this is your chance—leaving her book on the table. You wander over and pick it up. *Doggy Discipline: Better Pet Behaviour in Six Weeks*, but this was not what you expected. What a neat surprise and what an important thing for community members to have a space where they can come together and learn about each other in this exciting way. How remarkable it is to hold a book like *Doggy Discipline* which only seconds earlier was in the hands of a complete stranger. But is she a stranger? You know so much about her already: she's a library patron, a fellow reader, a pet owner. You sign up for a borrower's card and take the book home, running your fingers along its spine for the duration of the bus ride.

Later as you're sitting down to dinner, you notice the book on the edge of the table. A strange feeling passes through you, as if you're not alone. The pretty girl from the library is there too, by way of the book you have both held and enjoyed that very day. You lift *Doggy Discipline* to your nose and a lovely, floral scent wafts from its pages; this is the sweet aroma of your new friend. You caress the individual edges of the paper as you open the book, where her thumbs had turned the pages hours earlier and marvel at the intimacy of the library experience. You plant a kiss on the book's cover—right on the nose of the golden retriever in the photograph—and know that somewhere a pretty girl is swooning.

Throughout your meal you speak to the book as if *she* were there with you because, in a way she is. You tell her about your daily life as a parking attendant, your dreams of owning your own lot and how all your old friends had moved away years ago—the whole story. She is helpless but to listen. But how one-sided, you think, and so you turn to page thirty-five and extract a reply: "Make sure to use the choke-chain properly, or you may cause damage to your dog's throat/neck."

You bring the book to bed that night thinking you'll give it a read before drifting off. You lay on your back, letting your eyes fall upon the same words *her* eyes had studied so carefully in the library. By the time you reach the chapter on making your own punitive apple face-spray, your arms are too tired to hold the book upright any longer and so you lay it on the pillow beside your own. "Good night, pretty girl," you whisper and fall asleep with your hand between the pages.

The next day, you take the book to work and cram an extra stool into the attendant's booth for it to rest on. You prattle on about various things, read random passages from its pages when it's slow and before you know it, it's your lunch hour. How quickly a day passes when you don't have to spend it alone! You skip the food court for today and head to the library instead— maybe you'll see the pretty girl. The pretty girl is not there and so you return to the library every day that week—sometimes more than once—in the hopes that you'll run into her again. You bring *Doggy Discipline* with you each time so she'll notice you reading it and recognize a kindred spirit but the girl remains absent. The following Saturday morning, however, you see her pass by the library window.

In a panic, you shove the book into your bag and

run outside. You see her crossing the street at the end of the block and are almost flattened by a bus. You catch up and follow the pretty girl—just as you had done the first time you saw her—until you reach a bungalow by the river, just outside downtown. She goes inside while you stand behind a row of bushes to look at her little house. You hear a dog bark relentlessly inside and the occasional hiss of what you assume to be homemade face-spray. It's windy by the river and you begin to shiver in the cold. You remember the warmth of the library and the wonderful feeling of community you felt the first day you went in. What a simple, lovely thing: how two people, who otherwise might never have met, are able to cross paths amongst the stacks of books; how one of these people, now that the two are connected in this way, might ask the other to borrow a sweater when passing by on a chilly day; how it would be no big deal, should the passerby happen to be a bit shy, for him to simply grab a sweater from the clothesline in the other's backyard and continue on his way. You walk home in comfort, warmed by the kind offering of the pretty girl.

Once home, you remove the sweater and lay it out on your bed. Fetching *Doggy Discipline* from your bag, you stick the bottom of the book through the sweater's collar and squint. It looks just like the pretty girl. You lie down beside her and clutch one of her soft sleeves to your chest.

You don't see the pretty girl at the library anymore but occasionally you pass by her bungalow after work and watch from the bushes. Sometimes she steps outside with her dog, whose behaviour, you notice, is improving with each visit. What she's up to doesn't really matter though because everything you need is at home, lying on your bed. Someone you can rely on; someone who won't move away and leave you all alone; someone to watch movies and laugh and go for walks with. And you don't mind that you're obliged to bring your new companion back to the library for renewal every three weeks to avoid late fines. The love of *Doggy Discipline* may be on loan but you now know this: borrowed happiness is happiness nonetheless.

FOR HENRY

Susanne Beecher looks through the viewfinder at the crowd gathering below. She pans over people on blankets, in collapsible chairs or standing in front of food trucks waiting for elephant ears and ice cream. She zooms in on a fat man wiping his bald head with a napkin, sweaty. Henry'll get a kick out of this, she thinks.

"Look, my old boyfriend," she says.

Susanne adores fireworks in Heller Park on Victoria Day. Half the city coming together, sharing the evening. Everyone looking up at the sky, waiting. The smell of fried sugar. The music from the rides all jumbled together. Children running around. Susanne and her husband Henry would go together every year. They'd sit up on a hill adjacent to Heller Park and over-looking the Sage River. A little further away from the festivities, but not too far. It was private and the view was just as good if not better. You had to climb over a plastic fence. Their secret spot. This year, Henry was laid up in the hospital with late-stage lung cancer. *End* stage is what the doctors said, actually. She tried to convince her husband to come but the nurses said no way, out of the question. Henry deferred to them which was a shame. Of course, his health was the most important thing, his comfort. Still, a shame. Morale was important too. She read an article somewhere about a little boy who went into remission after going outside in his hospital gown for a snowball fight.

Susanne has a plan though. She's there, alone, with her video camera at their spot on the hill. The same blanket they always used laid out in the grass and her hair done up in a tight bun the way Henry likes it. His favourite red dress. She'll record the whole thing; capture the fireworks display on tape but not just that: the crowds, the river, everything. Susanne on camera herself. She'll talk to Henry as if he were there. It'll feel like he *is* there.

"All these people," Susanne says. The camera sweeps over the park. It's eight o'clock and the sun is fading. "Busier than ever, wouldn't you say? I'm so glad we have our special spot."

She lowers the camera to her lap. I should start over, she thinks. That joke about dating the fat man. First of all, it was cruel. The tape is supposed to lift Henry's spirits, not put people down. But also, the reference to dating other men—inappropriate considering what had happened. A month earlier, when Henry moved to palliative care, he confessed to Susanne that he'd had affairs. Plural. More than one affair. She'd had her suspicions but always put it out of her mind. I'm just being paranoid, she'd think. But it was true, there were other women and she couldn't do anything about it. It had happened. She couldn't even be angry with him because he's dying. Henry wanted her to lash out. Begged her to smack him around, to walk out on him.

But she couldn't; not with him lying in that bed. The affairs were upsetting but it was much more upsetting that he was dying. She had to let it go. It was her duty as his wife to make his final days, however many he has left, as pleasant as possible.

Susanne stops the recording and deletes the file. She starts over. Pans over the crowd again. No old boyfriend jokes this time. Instead, she zooms in on a dog barking at a trash can. She hears the sounds of laughter coming up the hill behind her. People are coming. She turns her head but keeps the camera steadily stationary—it's a group of teenage boys in hoodies, ball caps and backpacks. Four of them. Rat faces.

"Hey, lady," the tallest boy says. The others laugh. They hop the plastic fence and sit in the grass behind Susanne. She half-smiles at the tall boy and turns back around.

Perfect, she thinks. Cordoned off by the fence and a line of trees that stretch back into the yard of a daycare, the space at the top of the hill is small and intimate. The size of her living room, if that. The whole energy of the video is ruined. It won't feel like she's alone with Henry, the way it should feel, but there's nothing she can do. She can't move. This is the spot. She must press on, keep filming.

She hears backpack zippers unzip behind her. The boys are talking about weed or PlayStation, she can't tell. They all mumble and speak in some kind of teenage code. Someone's always laughing.

Susanne points her camera at the horizon. The last light of the sun setting behind the buildings downtown.

"The fireworks are starting real soon, honey," she says. She speaks softly so the boys won't hear her.

"She's talking to herself," a voice says.

"No, she's talking to *honey*."

"Shut up you guys. She's right there."

Susanne pauses the video. The boys are ruining her film. Henry won't want to hear all this. It'll only make him angry listening to these delinquents talk about his wife. He'll worry and Henry needs to relax. He has enough unpleasantness to deal with. She needs to say something, she realizes. She clears her throat.

"Excuse me," Susanne says, turning to the teen-agers. Four rat faces look up at once. All teeth and eyes. "I'm sorry to intrude but could you keep your voices down a touch?"

"Sure thing, honey," the tall one says. He stretches the word "honey" out mockingly. Everyone giggles.

"Thank you," Susanne says. She feels blood rushing to her cheeks. "I'm sorry to intrude."

She hits RECORD again and continues filming the horizon. She can't hold the camera steady because her hands are shaking. She presses PAUSE again and takes a deep breath, closes her eyes. She's missing important footage—the best part of watching fireworks was the build-up, the anticipation—but she'll have to wait until she's calm.

The boys are mumbling at a lower volume now. The giggling continues but Susanne can work with that.

A little laughter won't ruin the experience for Henry. She lifts the camera, steadies her hands and presses RECORD.

She focuses in on the Ferris wheel spinning below the hill. She and Henry went on that same Ferris wheel two years earlier. It wasn't all that big but she was nervous to get on. Henry had rubbed her shoulders in the queue. It was so romantic. They'd climbed into their seat with the bar on their laps, the ride had started and it was fine. She wasn't nervous at all because Henry was with her, because he'd rubbed her shoulders. And then, she remembers, Henry had pointed out a woman standing in line for the Gravitron. Said he knew her from work. Susanne can picture the woman now—she had worn a white tank top. Huge breasts. She could see that they were huge from the very top of the Ferris wheel. Was that one of the women Henry had slept with? Susanne thinks. Dear Lord, why do I have that memory? Why hold onto the image of some woman in a tank top?

She can't think about this right now, she realizes. She needs to stay in the moment. Immerse herself in the experience for Henry. She can deal with these memories later, when Henry's gone. She takes a breath and smiles. She turns the camera on herself.

"I'm so excited, Henry," she says and flips a stray lock of hair behind her ear. "I love you so much."

The teenagers erupt. Susanne turns to see them rolling on the ground clutching their sides.

"Oh my God," the tall one says, barely able to breathe.

"I love you so much, Henry!" another screams through the laughter.

Susanne hits PAUSE and stands up. Her hands shaking again, she fumbles with the camera but manages to grab the strap before the lens shatters on the ground.

"Please," she says to the boys who are still on the ground, laughing it up at her expense. "I asked you nicely. I'm trying to make a video for my husband. He's very sick. We can share this space but can you please be mindful?"

"We're sorry, miss," a boy with a horrible moustache says. He is out of breath. "We'll be quiet. Go ahead with your, uh, video."

"Thank you," Susanne says and sits back down. She closes her eyes. She takes slow, deep breaths.

It's not fair, she thinks. She and Henry always sat up on the hill. No one had ever joined them before. This spot was theirs. Henry wasn't there in person this time, so maybe she should count herself lucky that they had it to themselves all those years. But maybe it would have been better if the teenagers, those rats, had come up the hill another year when Henry was there too. He would have put them in their place, intimidated them. Henry wasn't a gladiator by any stretch, but he was big enough. Once when they were eating at Denny's some college kids in the next booth over were out of control. They were talking too loudly, cursing, telling obscene stories. It was ruining the meal and Henry was fuming. "Let's just move to another booth," Susanne had said, but Henry wouldn't have it. He'd stood up, put his hands down on their table and told them to pipe down. They did. He took control then and he'd have taken control of this situation too if he wasn't stuck in that awful hospital. Teach these kids some manners.

Now that she thinks of it, why didn't they just move to another booth? They were seated near the back of the restaurant with Henry facing away from the front entrance. Maybe he was worried one of his side-things would come in to the Denny's. One of his women. Like the one with the white top and big breasts. Every time she and Henry had gone out to eat, he'd likely scanned the room for her and any other girl-friends. He was probably a nervous wreck whenever they'd left the house together. And there was Susanne, oblivious, thinking they were having fun.

Susanne picks up the camera and resumes filming. She can't think like this, it's selfish. Poor Henry is all alone in his tiny room, staring up a TV bolted to the wall, coughing up blood every five minutes and here she is complaining about the past. Speculating. She'll toughen up and get through this. The boys are quieter now. Still muttering away but the incessant giggling seems to have stopped. Susanne focuses in on a little girl running across the park with sparklers in both hands.

"Look at her go," she whispers.

She follows the girl as she weaves through the crowd. Henry will love this, she knows. Such a beautiful shot. The little girl perfectly captures the spirit of the evening. She runs past the groups of people huddled by the riverbank and through a sea of canvas chairs. She's easy to track because of the sparklers.

A large blurry face appears in the camera's view-finder taking up the whole screen.

"Hi, honey!" the face says.

Susanne drops the camera and screams. Her heart is pounding in her chest, in her throat. It's one of the teenagers, the tall one. He'd crept over the fence, walked down the hill until he was out of sight and then snuck up on her, the rat. The little shit. The boys are howling behind her.

"Hey!" Susanne says. She lunges forward on her knees and grabs the tall kid by his sleeve. "You little shit."

"Calm down," the boy says. "We're joking around."

She smacks him across the face with the back of her hand.

"No," she says. "*You* calm down, you rat. I asked you to be quiet. You can't leave me alone? No?"

Susanne pushes the kid. Shoves him hard. He falls back down the hill a few feet and hits the plastic fence.

"And you!" She turns to the three other boys behind her on the grass. She hears a shrill whistling noise in the distance. The boys look up at her, their faces worried. The whistling noise gets louder and louder. Then a crack across the sky, an explosion. The fireworks. Her whole body is shaking.

"I asked you to be quiet!" She's not sure if the boys can hear her over the sound of the fireworks. There's an explosion every few seconds but she lets them have it anyway. "You're not supposed to be here, you rat kids. This is our spot and you're goddamn intruding. You little rat intruders. No respect for anyone and you think you can do whatever you damn well please without consequence, without consideration for other people's feelings. Well, get the fuck off my hill!"

She reaches down and grabs one of the kid's backpacks in her hands. She tosses it and it almost hits the tall kid in the head who is still lying in shock along the fence she'd pushed him into. She makes for another backpack but the teenagers scoop everything they can into their arms and run off like little rat cowards.

Susanne looks at the kids scurrying away down the hill. The sky is full of colour and smoke. The whistling, screaming, cracking noises of the fireworks continue. No one notices the commotion atop the hill because everyone's looking up at the fireworks. Susanne's throat stings. All that shouting. Her hand stings too.

Susanne's camera is lying on the grass. She kneels down and picks it up. It's still recording. Would it have captured her yelling over the sound of the fireworks? She isn't sure. She presses PAUSE. Then the STOP button. She sits down.

She feels good. Light. Floaty. I came all this way, she thinks. Got all dolled up. She lifts the camera once again and hits RECORD. She'll finish the video. Her original idea had been ruined by those damn kids but maybe this is exactly what Henry needs to see. She hopes the audio of her screaming is clear. She wants her husband to hear all of it, every word.

The pauses between explosions are getting longer. Quiet stretches, building anticipation toward the finale.

"Isn't this beautiful, honey?" Susanne says and turns the camera on herself, smiling. "I just love it here." She hits PAUSE, leans back on her elbows and looks up at the sky.

SELF-GUIDED MEDITATION

'm sitting in my most comfortable chair by the window that looks out onto the street. A cool breeze trickles in and I am calm. My eyes are closed. My breathing is slow and even and as I settle into this state of quietude and reflection, I begin to drift away.

I have left my attic apartment. I can no longer hear the traffic outside or my elderly landlord's TV blaring from the room below. The bills piling up on my kitchen table and the divorce papers from Wendy, still unsigned—they don't exist. I'm on my island.

The temperature on my island is perfect today. It's always perfect. It's warm but not too warm. I can walk across the sand without flip-flops and there are no sunburns. I can lay out on the beach all day if I want without the threat of skin cancer. Negative phrases like "skin cancer" don't make sense on my island—say it and people will look at you funny. No mosquitoes here either. Only butterflies. It's sunny and quiet and it never rains on my island unless I want it to. I am in control.

Right now, I am alone on my island. I have it all to myself. If I get lonely, however, I simply snap my fingers and a cruise ship will dock nearby. The friendliest people in the world will step off the boat and join me on the beach. They are celebrities, beautiful women and award-winning chefs. The celebrities update me on the latest Hollywood gossip and tell me racy stories. The beautiful women compliment me and then have sex with me. The chefs cook me omelettes. I have sex with the celebrities too, and sometimes even the chefs. And if I feel like being alone again I whistle and the cruise ship returns to pick everyone up.

Wendy isn't allowed on my island. There's a special passport you must have to visit my island that only wealthy people can afford. She can't bang on my beach hut door in the morning, pleading with me to sign the divorce papers. Her lawyer can't call me—I don't have a phone here. There's no need. I have telepathic powers and I can "talk" to whomever I want by thinking at them. I have my twenty-five-year-old body, which isn't bad, and my eighteen-year-old hairline. Not bad at all.

Except today, I feel like seeing Wendy. Maybe I miss her. I just don't want her to look at me with that concerned, pitying stare she sometimes gives me. But this is my island and Wendy can't give me unwanted looks here. I'm the boss. I teleport a special passport to Wendy and the cruise ship drops her off.

I see Wendy walking down the beach towards me with her bags. She's smiling. I'm breathing slowly, in through the nose, out through the mouth. I am calm. Should I be helping Wendy with her luggage? She looks upset.

"I'm coming, Wendy!" I shout to her. "Put those heavy bags down. I'm on my way!"

As I run towards my estranged wife, I trip and spill my mai tai in the sand.

"Look at you," Wendy sighs. "Still with the mai tais? It's morning for Christ's sake. You're a mess."

"I'm sorry, Wendy," I say. "I'll stop drinking, I promise. I'm ready to change."

But I'm not sorry. I like mai tais and this is my island. I can drink as much as I want to because there are no consequences to drinking as much as I want to on my island. No hangovers. I don't call people up from my past at three in the morning and sob into the phone. I don't drive over to my wife's new apartment building and set fire to old photo albums in the parking lot— there's none of that. I can drink all day, mai tai after mai tai, and relax in the sun.

Wendy is crying a little with her hands over her face but I remember that this is just my imagination. I can change things. When an undesirable thought passes through my mind, it's important to recognize it as such—simply a momentary, passing thought—and then let it float away like a helium balloon. Wendy is gone.

Maybe she's still on the island though, somewhere nearby. I'd like her to be around in case we find a way to work things out. She'd really enjoy the island if she gave it a chance. She was always complaining that we never got to go on vacations, that I'd go alone on business trips and drink myself into a coma and that she didn't ever get to go anywhere. Well, here you are, Wendy! The most stunning, luxurious tropical island my mind can conjure. I correspond telepathically with my real estate agent and buy Wendy her own beach hut, just around the cove. That way I can keep an eye on her. Make sure she's safe.

I walk over to Wendy's beach hut to check on her. Her beach hut is quite nice. Nicer than mine, actually. It's much bigger and stands on tall poles so the tide doesn't come in and flood her place, which happens nightly over at my beach hut. Anyway, I scramble up a tree and peek inside her bedroom window to see if she's okay.

Wait, what's Dr. Hoffman doing in there? If we're separated, why does Wendy still need to see our marriage counsellor? Maybe she wants to reconcile. Maybe he's trying to convince her to take me back. But then why is he taking off her clothes?

Shit.

They're having sex. They're really going at it. Wendy's having sex with our marriage counsellor in the deluxe beach hut I just bought for her with the drapes wide open, to mock me. Dr. Hoffman looks up from the bed and winks at me—winks! Was this his plan all along? Was this why he taught Wendy and I self-guided meditation? So he could infiltrate my thoughts, show me he could do a better job of satisfying my wife in bed? Wendy's making a wild, intense moaning sound I've never heard before.

Breathe in through the nose and out through the mouth. I am in control.

This is my island.

A cruise ship docks and Academy Award–winning actress Jennifer Lawrence comes running up the beach and climbs into my tree. We're going to have sex right here on this branch so Wendy and Dr. Hoffman can see how it's really done. Jennifer Lawrence looks amazing in her coconut bra although now that I think of it, isn't Jennifer Lawrence kind of young for me? Not sure. I don't want to be a creep or anything. Maybe I'll quickly pop out of the meditation and Google Jennifer Lawrence's age—no WiFi on the island. Be right back.

I'm back. Internet's been cut off, I guess, but no matter. I was mistaken. It's actually Jennifer *Aniston* who got off the cruise ship and scurried up into my tree. She's definitely age appropriate and just as sexy. Alright, here we go.

"Hold on," Jennifer Aniston says. "I forgot my wallet."

"What do you need your wallet for?" I say, but she's already climbing down.

While I'm waiting, I teleport a mai tai into my hand and take a long, cool sip. Much better. On my island, drinking seven or eight mai tais doesn't affect my sexual performance whatsoever. I can throw back twenty and, if anything, my abilities only increase. I won't pass out on top of a lover either and I certainly won't vomit all over the bed. I'm ready to go.

Except now Jennifer Aniston is in the room with Wendy and Dr. Hoffman. I see her taking off her coconut bra before my marriage counsellor shuts the drapes.

Goddammit.

I revoke Wendy's special passport. I revoke Dr.

Hoffman's passport and I revoke Jennifer Aniston's passport too, which is a shame. They're all escorted onto the cruise ship and just like that, they're gone. I don't need to spy on Wendy. It doesn't matter what she's up to. I've moved on. I'm fine. I have my island.

I climb down from the tree and go back to my beach hut. While I was away some villagers—all beautiful women who just moved to the island and are nice to me and make me omelettes—put my beach hut up on poles and tidied the place and fixed the wooden floor, which was warped from constant flooding. They also put up a fence and security lights in case Wendy and Dr. Hoffman sneak back onto the island somehow. There's a large dog standing guard and the dog loves me unconditionally.

The villagers finally sorted out island WiFi and so I sit down at the computer in my beach hut and play online poker. Sometimes I relieve stress by playing online poker and sometimes I relieve stress by meditating. Why not combine the two? Sometimes the island itself is stressful and so I play online poker and I'm winning. Wendy thought I took online poker too far and ruined our financial security by making outlandish bets while I was drunk but now I'm winning. If only she could see me now. I win a game and I win another one and I'm drinking mai tais and everything is perfect.

Wait, what's that sound?

Wendy's banging on the door to my attic apartment. It could only be her—no one else ever comes by. But I'm not in my attic apartment. I'm on my island sipping a mai tai. And when I hear her violent, real-world knocking here on the island, it isn't the sound of Wendy trying to get in and force me to sign the divorce papers, it's the sound of the bedpost banging against the wall of my beach hut as I have sex with a beautiful celebrity chef who just made me an omelette. We're making love like wild dogs and the louder Wendy knocks, the more pleasure I'm giving this gorgeous, adoring woman. In fact, this woman isn't a famous chef at all—it's Wendy. She's taken me back and we're going at it and the bed sounds like it's about to break. Don't stop Wendy. We can do this. She's not pleading with me to let her in so we can "finalize this damn thing," her voice muffled by the door. She's pleading with me to stay here, in my beach hut on the island, making love and drinking mai tais all day.

"I never wanted a divorce," she says. "The whole thing was a test and you passed. You passed with flying colours, dear."

"You can stay, Wendy," I say. "You can move in today. We'll live here on the island together and everything will be perfect. Just don't stop knocking. Don't stop."

And when I finally open my eyes, the knocking has stopped and Wendy is gone but I'm smiling. The meditation is over. Everything will be okay. I walk to the kitchen and fix myself a mai tai because even though it's only ten in the morning, I'm on island time.

MRS. FLOOD WAS HERE

When Mrs. Flood awoke Saturday morning in her car, she refused to believe it. I can't be here, she thought. I'm in my bed. Mother will knock shortly. She'll put on the radio and I'll scramble the eggs.

She unfastened her seatbelt and opened the door. It would only swing out a few inches—there were branches in the way. She was parked in a forest. She leaned over and threw up in the snow, through the crack in the door. She wiped her mouth on her coat sleeve. Why would I sleep in the car? she thought. It didn't make any sense. I've slept in the same bed forever. In Mother's house. No trips, no vacations. Mrs. Flood could remember spending the night in a hotel years ago, when she went to her cousin's wedding up north. Fifteen years ago? Twenty? But that's it. There's no reason I'd be in the woods, she decided. I'll wake up soon. She lay back in her chair and closed her eyes.

Mrs. Flood awoke a second time. Before she opened her eyes she could feel the cold window against her cheek. She was sitting upright in a vinyl seat. She could smell the car.

She remembered that last night there was a raucous gathering at the house next door to her and

Mother. She had lain in bed, balling her fists. Those awful Milner kids back from college for the winter break, parties every other night. Normally she'd have put up with the noise but she had to get up early the next day. Oh God, she was missing the funeral. The funeral was *today*.

The Milner kids, Mrs. Flood remembered. The loud music, the booming voices, the idiotic laughter. She'd screamed and screamed, pacing around her bedroom. She'd looked at the telephone but couldn't bring herself to call the cops. She certainly couldn't have stormed over there herself. What, in her bathrobe? She'd gotten in the car and set out in the hopes of finding a room at a motel nearby. She was driving down Pine Road, above the ravine. She'd hit a patch of ice.

Now here she was at the bottom of the ravine below Pine Road, most likely. She didn't think she'd been terribly injured—she was just cold, nauseous—but sometimes you're in shock and you can't tell. She opened her eyes to check for bruises and gashes in the rear-view mirror when something else caught her attention. A shape on the hood of the car. There was a long crack running down the middle of the windshield. A thin layer of ice on the glass distorted her view, but she could see the shape. A shape with a long face. It was looking at her.

But that couldn't be, Mrs. Flood decided, and so she closed her eyes again. It's one of those nasty dreams where you think you're awake when you're not. Soon she'd get up and start on those scrambled eggs. Mother would put on the radio. "Jimmy Mack" or "Chain Gang." They'd dance around the kitchen.

Mrs. Flood knew exactly what the shape was—a wolf. She opened her eyes. It was really there. On the hood of the car, looking in at her. It was massive. Just sitting there, staring. She didn't know there were wolves in the area. Coyotes, sure. Just last week the mail carrier was saying that she ought to keep her cat inside on account of a coyote skulking around. Mrs. Flood had thanked him but didn't tell him that she didn't own a cat.

A wolf on the hood. Or perhaps it was a dog, she thought. One of those sled dogs or some kind of mix. But no, she could tell it was a wolf. It wasn't like looking at a photograph, which can be iffy. This creature on her hood had a presence. Its eyes said "wolf." She couldn't leave the car. She couldn't dial for help either—no cellphone. She and her mother shared a landline. No one called them, they figured. They rarely left the house so what was the use?

Mrs. Flood turned the key in the ignition; the engine hummed. The wolf's ears perked up like two menacing little triangles. She couldn't drive straight ahead because there were trees in the way. She turned on the heat, then spun around to look through the back window. The car was pitched forward and now she could see why: she was parked at the bottom of a hill at the ravine. Her back tires were on the slope. Her Sunbird would never make it. A pile of fresh snow covered whatever tracks she'd made coming down. Pale light shone through the patches of trees on the hill; it was early morning. Surely someone would drive by and see the broken guardrail along Pine Road.

Except there wasn't a guardrail. Mother always went on about that when Mrs. Flood dropped her off at bridge club, or when they went out to the Applebee's together. "It's criminal," her mother would say. "They ought to call this stretch Lawsuit Lane." No smashed-up guardrail to signal passersby, a thick layer of snow hiding everything. And then there was the wolf. Someone would find her, she knew. Soon enough. Soon, soon, soon.

The wolf opened its jaws as if it might speak, like it was her spirit guide, but it only yawned. Long, white teeth and blackish gums.

"Jesus!" Mrs. Flood exclaimed. She pressed her hand into the centre of the steering wheel and blasted the horn.

The wolf stood up and leaned towards the windshield, its eyes locked on Mrs. Flood. She pushed the horn again and the wolf let out a high-pitched moan like a balloon releasing air. It squealed while Mrs. Flood pressed down on the horn. Wolves aren't supposed to make noises like this, she thought. It was drooling. A thin rope of saliva swung from the wolf's jaw as it continued to moan. The animal was deranged. Mentally challenged. Rabid. One of its eyes wandered to the side of the eyelid as though it were having a seizure.

"Go away!" said Mrs. Flood. "Get out of here!"

The wolf crouched down low and began licking

the windshield. Mrs. Flood released the horn. The wolf's tongue streaked across the glass. Mrs. Flood pressed her palms into her eyes and sunk back into her seat. Those goddamn Milner kids. No consideration for other people. I'll goddamn kill those Milner kids.

A minute passed and the terrible squeaking of the wolf's tongue stopped. Still, Mrs. Flood pushed her hands into her face again, the blood rushing to her eye sockets. The funeral was today. Mother's funeral. She needed to be there for her mother. She needed all this to stop, whatever this was.

When she looked up again, the wolf was gone. There were wet streaks all over the windshield and large paw prints on the hood, but no wolf. In the rear-view, she saw the gash on her forehead and dried blood in her bangs. There was a sharp pain in her right leg and she had a pulsing headache. Most of all, though, she was thirsty. Mrs. Flood felt around in the backseat but knew there wouldn't be anything to drink there. She kept a tidy car and a spotless bedroom. She looked out the window—snow. There were piles of it. She could eat the snow.

Her door wouldn't open wide enough, and besides, there was vomit on the other side. Mrs. Flood shifted to the passenger seat and looked out the window. No sign of the wolf. She'd have to be sure though.

She tapped the horn, twice. No wolf.

Slowly, she pushed the passenger door open—just a crack—and scooped a handful of snow. She closed the door and filled her mouth. Instant relief. Her whole body tingled, like she'd eaten a bowl of sugar. She devoured the entire scoop, then licked her hands. Her fingers were numb. Still thirsty, she opened the door again and took another handful. Again, she licked her hands clean.

Mrs. Flood rubbed her hands between her legs to warm them after holding the snow. She heard a thump and then the vehicle lurched. She looked up. The wolf was back. It sat down on the hood of the car and looked in at her.

"No," Mrs. Flood said. "Get out of here."

She leaned forward and dropped her head between her legs. Her jeans were damp around the thighs from her hands. The heat was on but she was shaking. She kept her head down, eyes closed and hands down by the floor grasping her ankles. If I wait, it'll leave, she thought. Someone will come. She could hear the wolf licking the glass above her.

A few minutes passed and the wolf jumped down and trotted off. Mrs. Flood watched it disappear into the bushes ahead. If I make a run for it, she thought, I could try and scale the ravine. Climb up to the road and flag someone down. It was a steep climb and if the wolf came back, good lord. Those awful teeth.

Mrs. Flood remembered the CD player in the glove compartment and plugged it into the dashboard. The digital clock flashed ten thirty. The funeral was at noon at Poletti & Sons Funeral Home out on Antrim Road.

A small service since Mrs. Flood's mother had few friends. There were the women from her bridge club, though they hadn't spoken in years and her old boss at the cereal factory, Mr. Raebos, had been notified. It was likely that at least one of the ladies from the assembly line would show up. As far as family, there wasn't much left. Her mother hadn't spoken to her brother in ages due to an ancient rift Mrs. Flood had never fully understood. Grandma and Grandpa were long gone. After Mrs. Flood discovered her mother on the bathroom floor with the empty pill bottles, there had been very few phone calls she'd needed to make.

At the very least, Mr. Poletti or one of his sons would notice Mrs. Flood's absence. She had their cheque. How soon before they called the police? she wondered. How soon before someone organized a search party?

She had to pee. Squatting beside the car was risky—the wolf could return at any moment. There wasn't anything in the car she could use as a receptacle. Her purse would work, but then she'd ruin her purse. She dug around inside her bag and settled on her sunglass case. Setting the case on the seat below her, Mrs. Flood reclined the seat back and propped herself up on her elbows. It wasn't easy. It took considerable concentration to release her bladder in such an awkward position and she soon realized the sunglass case wasn't big enough. She had to stop mid-stream, check the windows for the wolf, pour the case's contents out into the snow and reposition herself before she could finish. She filled the case four times. The car smelled like urine.

She watched the clock. Ten forty-five passed by, then eleven. She ate more snow. Nobody came to her rescue.

At eleven twenty, the wolf returned. It jumped on the hood again but this time it had something in its mouth. A dead rabbit. The wolf dropped the rabbit next to the windshield wipers and leapt back down. It looked into Mrs. Flood's eyes as it walked by the window, tongue lolling from the side of its mouth, and slunk back into the woods.

A gift. The wolf doesn't want to hurt me, Mrs. Flood thought. It's feeding me. Or fattening me up. I'm already fat, though. She closed her eyes.

An hour passed. The wolf hadn't returned and Mrs. Flood was still nauseous and only getting worse—she couldn't stomach looking at the dead rabbit in the windshield much longer. Its white fur stained with blood, one leg contorted at an ungodly angle.

I don't care if I get attacked, Mrs. Flood thought. I don't care if the wolf rips out my throat and leaves me bleeding in the snow. I'm not sitting here another minute. I'm going home.

She turned off the car and put the keys back in her pocket. She picked up her purse, opened the passenger door and stepped over her urine into fresh snow. The slope was steeper than she'd thought; she couldn't see the road through the trees. How she'd survived the crash was perplexing. She looked at the car and saw the back bumper was missing. The trunk was crumpled up and there were a few long scratches along the side. There was a smell of gasoline in the air, otherwise the car wasn't in such bad shape, considering the fall.

There wasn't any kind of path. She stepped through snow up to her knees and kicked through bramble. The wolf wasn't in sight. Her head was buzzing. Her legs throbbed with pain but she had to get up to the road.

"Please," she whispered. "Please let me go home." She hadn't spoken to God since she was a child and Mother dragged her to church. She wasn't sure it was God she was reaching out to now. Any benevolent force that would listen would do. If she made it out of this alive, she promised to repent. She'd look over her life—really scrutinize everything she'd said and done— and make up for whatever ethical missteps she'd made along the way. Her mother, for one. She knew Mother had a problem with prescription pills. She saw how she relied on them but had said nothing. Enabled her. They enabled each other, really. Two spinsters, mother and daughter, wasting away in that house.

You better stay in tonight, Mrs. Flood would say. You're too sick for bridge club.

And then Mother would say You're late when Mrs. Flood didn't make it home from the office by five-thirty exactly. You've let me down. I need you here, I need you to take care of me. Maybe this job of yours isn't such a good idea.

Mrs. Flood trudged through the snow. There was

the threat of the wolf returning but she could only walk so fast. Her legs throbbed and her feet were soaking wet and freezing. She felt dizzy and close to fainting. Soon she came to a large oak that had fallen over against the slope that she might be able to use to help her climb up. If she made it up to the roots there was a long stretch of grass the snow hadn't touched that would be easier to traverse. She couldn't see past the trees and didn't know if it would take her right to the road, but this was her best option. She held on to the oak and started her way up. Midway up the trunk, she became aware of a familiar shape in her periphery—the wolf. Above her on the slope, looking down. Its head was cocked at a strange angle, muzzle covered in a goatee of snow and mud. This is it, Mrs. Flood thought. I'm coming, Mother.

The wolf took a step towards her. Mrs. Flood stepped backwards still holding the trunk. She couldn't turn around and show the wolf her back, a sign of weakness. The wolf took another step. Mrs. Flood took a step. They kept a steady, gradual pace. Soon, she was back at the bottom of the ridge. The wolf came down on her right side and walked her towards the car. Herding her like a sheepdog.

Mrs. Flood was exhausted, dizzy and numb with pain but she kept walking backwards. Eventually they made it back to the car. Mrs. Flood opened the passenger door and climbed in to the smell of urine, the disfigured rabbit. When she was back in place with the door shut, the wolf jumped up onto the hood.

For an hour, Mrs. Flood sat with her eyes closed while the wolf licked the glass before she heard it jump down. When she opened her eyes, the rabbit was gone. She realized then that nobody was coming. This is where I live. This is where I'll die. There's nothing I can do but wait.

Mrs. Flood pictured her empty, quiet home. It was different without Mother in there, as if all the bricks had been replaced one by one. Mother was her world. Sometimes it had felt like they were the last two people on the planet, carrying the torch for humanity. And now Mother was gone. Soon Mrs. Flood would be gone too. The end of the world.

She pressed play on the CD console. Sam Cooke's *Greatest Hits*. Much too merry for the situation. All those major chords. She turned it off and reached into her purse and pulled out a pen and a gas receipt. She thought about writing a note for whoever eventually found her to explain what happened. Some kind of final message. After some thought she settled on "Mrs. Flood was here." She pushed the note into her pocket.

A few minutes later, the vehicle lurched.

Mrs. Flood squinted at the beast on her hood. You shouldn't be here, she thought. Why do you keep coming back? Why can't you leave me the fuck alone? She punched the horn. The wolf stood up. It was an ugly thing, a coward. Were its legs trembling? An ugly, idiotic thing with shaky legs.

To hell with it, thought Mrs. Flood. She ejected

the full CD player. The little screen went blank. The time was irrelevant now. There would be no funeral.

The CD player had weight to it. Like Mother's golden swan doorstop. Mrs. Flood rolled down the passenger window. The wolf stared.

"Go on!" Mrs. Flood said.

She leaned over the window's edge and sent the CD player flying. It hit the wolf in the chest. The wolf yelped and shuffled back with its tail between its legs.

"Get out of here! Go!"

The wolf began squealing again—that same obnoxious balloon whine.

Mrs. Flood threw her glasses case next but missed. She tossed her wallet—it struck the wolf in the snout. Then she threw her entire purse. The wolf jumped down and out of view. Mrs. Flood reached into the back seat and found Mother's Sunoco umbrella. Stepped out of the car.

"Where are you?" she said.

The wolf cowered beside a bush, its head down low. It looked smaller now. Like a big housecat, she thought.

"Go on," Mrs. Flood said. "Get lost."

She wielded the umbrella high over her head and approached. The wolf looked up with dumb, glossy eyes.

She brought the umbrella down hard, striking the wolf in the face with the metal tip. The wolf yelped. She struck again and the wolf backed away, a confused, maybe even hurt look on its face.

"Go!"

She followed the animal, brandishing her umbrella. The wolf began to trot. Mrs. Flood flung the umbrella like a javelin in the wolf's direction. The umbrella opened mid-air and became caught in a tree branch.

Mrs. Flood coughed and fell to her knees, plunged her hands into the snow. She vomited and rolled onto her back, spread out on top of the vomit. She wiped her mouth on her shoulder and closed her eyes. I'm in my bed, she thought. I'm in my car. I'm in my bed and my bed's in my car and maybe I'll just lay here a few more minutes.

Mrs. Flood was being carried on a yellow stretcher. Two women were there in black uniforms. There were other people around too. Lights flashed. There were voices. Something was on her neck—she couldn't move her head. There were ropes. She was being carried up the hill. One of the women said, "Keep her steady." Muffled radio voices in the background.

"Mother's funeral," Mrs. Flood said.

"What did she say?" one of the women said.

"Something about her mother," the other said.

"You'll see your mother soon," the first woman said. "We're taking you to the hospital. Everything's going to be alright."

"No I won't," Mrs. Flood said. She wouldn't see her mother again.

Lights and voices. The wolf nearby, standing

perfectly still. Listening and smelling. Hidden in the trees. Then slouching away; moving slowly, like a depressed child. Turning its head back to Mrs. Flood now and again.

ACKNOWLEDGEMENTS

Earlier versions of these stories originally appeared in the following publications: "Blind Man" in *The New Quarterly*, "Cop House" in *The Puritan*, "New Ice Kingdom" in *Prism International*, "Frank" in *The Dalhousie Review*, "Sketch Artist, Boxer, Party Planner, Baker" in *Joyland* and *Retro 4*, "This Deer Won't Look Both Ways" in *McSweeney's Internet Tendency*, "The Girl Who Smelled of Sarsaparilla" in *The Feathertale Review*, "DeRosa" in *Joyland*, "Spirit Pals" in *Carousel*, "The Fiddler Murders" in *Prism International*, "Pool Rules" in *McSweeney's Internet Tendency*, "Ode to the Library" in *The Rusty Toque*, "For Henry" in *Grain*, "Self-Guided Meditation" in *The Feathertale Review* and "Mrs. Flood Was Here" in *The Fiddlehead*. Thank you to the editors of each.

KATIE SHELSTAD

Sam Shelstad's work has appeared in many literary journals including *The Fiddlehead, PRISM international, The Puritan* and *McSweeney's.* The title story of *Cop House* was a runner-up for the Thomas Morton Memorial Prize in 2014. Shelstad lives in Toronto, Ontario.